Praise for

To Brew or Not to Brew

"Joyce Tremel's debut novel is cleverly developed, infused with fascinating details of craft brewing plus the very real flavor of Pittsburgh, and distilled into a unique and charming mystery. A delicious blend of strong characters and smooth delivery, *To Brew or Not to Brew* is sure to appeal to mystery readers and beer aficionados alike."

—Jennie Bentley, *New York Times* bestselling author of the Do-It-Yourself Mysteries

"A heartwarming blend of suds and suspense, featuring a determined heroine and her big Irish family. Tremel knows and loves her Pittsburgh setting, making the mystery all the more real and enjoyable."

—Cleo Coyle, *New York Times* bestselling author of the Coffeehouse Mysteries

"This charming debut novel stands out with a brewery setting that offers a unique twist on typical books within the genre. An assorted mix of characters provide a diverting dose of humor, flirtation, and heart. Between the peek into the brewing industry and the mouthwatering food descriptions, readers may find themselves scurrying to their nearest pub even while the baffling case compels them to devour just one more chapter!" —*RT Book Reviews* (Top Pick)

A ROOM
WITH A
Brew

JOYCE TREMEL

BERKLEY PRIME CRIME
New York

BERKLEY PRIME CRIME
Published by Berkley
An imprint of Penguin Random House LLC
375 Hudson Street, New York, New York 10014

ISBN: 9780425277713

First Edition: October 2017

Printed in the United States of America
3   5   7   9   10   8   6   4   2

Cover art by Bruce Emmett
Book design by Kristin del Rosario

To Layla,
who was possibly the best cat ever
and the inspiration for Hops.

R.I.P. 2004–2016.

ACKNOWLEDGMENTS

I can hardly believe this is the third book already! It seems like yesterday that I got the call from my agent that Berkley wanted to publish the Brewing Trouble series. I have so many people to thank for this wonderful adventure.

First and foremost, I want to thank my awesome agent, Myrsini Stephanides, at the Carol Mann Agency. None of this would have happened without her. She has been a great supporter and champion of my work and I'm truly lucky to be working with her.

I'd also like to thank my editor, Kristine Swartz. She has been a joy to work with, and really knows her stuff.

I can't forget the rest of the Penguin Random House staff. I don't know what I'd do without the copyeditors. Their knowledge of grammar and punctuation alone puts me to shame. Somehow they manage to make sense of some of my gibberish. And the art department! I have been so pleased with all of my covers. They are truly works of art—they bring the books to life. Thank you also to publicist Roxanne Jones, who is always quick to answer my questions and help me get the word out.

ACKNOWLEDGMENTS

Once again, I need to thank brewers Scott Smith at East End Brewing and Shawn Setzenfand at Hofbrauhaus Pittsburgh. They never hesitate to answer my sometimes stupid questions. Plus they make great beer!

I also want to send out a huge thank-you to all the book bloggers and reviewers who have read and reviewed the books in this series. I'd list them all by name, but I'm sure I'd miss someone and feel horrible about it. These bloggers do what they do because they love books and want to tell everyone about them. They have my undying gratitude.

Last, but certainly not least, I'd like to thank my family—especially my husband, Jerry. I couldn't do any of this without his love and support.

I hope "yinz guys" enjoy reading *A Room with a Brew* as much as I enjoyed writing it.

Prost!

CHAPTER ONE

$\mathfrak{I}$ slid onto an old piano stool as Daisy Hart placed the fall centerpiece she'd designed on the distressed wood counter in her flower shop, Beautiful Blooms.

"That looks great," I said. "It's exactly what I had in mind."

"When you said something for Oktoberfest," Daisy said, "I wasn't sure whether to go with autumn, beer, or Germany, so I looked it up and incorporated all of them."

"Well, it's perfect."

Daisy clapped her hands together, making her blond braids sway. Her choice of hairstyle made her look fifteen instead of in her early thirties. "I'm so glad."

It really was perfect. She'd used the traditional Oktoberfest colors of blue and white. The centerpiece sample consisted of cream-colored silk mums and blue asters, and in

1

the center was a miniature German beer stein. I'd ordered fourteen of them—enough to dress up all the tables in my brewpub. In two weeks, the Allegheny Brew House would be hosting its first Oktoberfest weekend.

Daisy came around the counter and took a seat on the other piano stool. "Explain one thing to me, Max. You're having this celebration in September. Shouldn't something called Oktoberfest happen in October?"

It was a common misconception. "The official Oktoberfest in Germany begins in mid-September and lasts for about two weeks. So it ends in October. Besides, Septemberfest doesn't have quite the same ring to it."

Daisy grinned. "No, it doesn't. How come you're wimping out and only having yours for a weekend?"

I laughed. "I'm having enough trouble coordinating everything for just the weekend. Do you know how hard it is to find an oompah band?"

"I never thought of that. But you did find one, right?"

"Yes," I said. "Candy, Kristie, and I are going to hear them play and make the final arrangements tonight. Why don't you come with us?"

"I don't know . . ."

"It'll be fun. A Friday girls' night out." I didn't add that she needed to get out and do something besides work on flower arrangements. She'd gone through a rough patch last spring when the man she'd been in love with had turned out to be someone who didn't care for her at all, and much worse. My insides still turned cold when I thought about what he'd done. Daisy had been devastated when she learned the truth and had even considered closing her shop and moving away. She was gradually becoming more like the old Daisy, but still had a little way to go.

She hesitated a moment, then said, "Maybe I will. It does sound like fun."

We talked for a few more minutes and decided I'd pick her up at eight. I was glad she'd agreed to go with us.

And it would be fun. Candy and Kristie would be sure to bring Daisy out of her self-imposed shell. Candy Sczypinski owned the bakery named Cupcakes N'at, which sat between the brewpub and Beautiful Blooms on Butler Street in the Lawrenceville neighborhood of Pittsburgh. The name of the bakery usually confused visitors to the city, but Candy never seemed to tire of explaining that *n'at* was really a shortened form of *and all that*. It was one of the expresssions commonly known as Pittsburghese.

Candy was a Pittsburgher—or Yinzer as natives were sometimes called—through and through. I'd never seen her wear any colors but black and gold, and I always thought she looked like Mrs. Santa Claus in Steelers garb. Despite being in her early seventies, she had more energy than a twenty-year-old.

Kristie Brinkley was the owner and barista at Jump, Jive & Java, the coffee shop across the street. She bore no resemblance to the supermodel, whose first name began with a *C*. Kristie looked more like Halle Berry, especially since she'd recently sheared off her dreadlocks and now only had a few streaks of purple in her hair. Purple this week anyway. She changed her hair color as often as some people changed their socks. I had a sneaking suspicion that her recent hairstyle change had something to do with the new love interest that she denied having. Candy was on the case, though. If anyone could discover who it was, she could.

As I passed the bakery on the way back to the brew house, Candy's assistant, Mary Louise, waved to me and I returned her wave. I was tempted to stop in for a treat, but I had a batch of stout in the brew kettle and it was time to get it ready for the fermentation tank. The Allegheny Brew House had been open since May, but I still got a thrill every time I neared the building. Its redbrick exterior with the large windows was exactly how I had pictured it would look when I bought the former office building of the defunct Steel City Brewery. It had been a true labor of love gutting and restoring the building. It hadn't been without its challenges and tragedies, but it was now everything I'd dreamed it would be.

Inside the pub, my staff was preparing for the lunch rush, and delicious aromas emanated from the kitchen. Nicole Clark, my part-time manager, was stacking glasses behind the polished dark oak bar, so I stopped to see her.

"Everything okay?" I asked.

"Yep." She nodded her head toward the brewery. "Need any help in there?"

Nicole was studying for her master's in chemistry at the University of Pittsburgh, and she'd taken a shine to the brewing process. She reminded me a lot of myself, although I'd been more interested in distilling when I earned my degree. That had only changed to brewing when I made a trip to Germany.

"Sure, as long as I'm not taking you from anything else."

The brewery portion of the brew house was to my left. I had

4

a 10-barrel or bbl system, which consisted of a mash tun to mash the malt grain, a brew kettle, and five fermentation tanks. In other words, I could brew approximately three hundred gallons at a time. It sounds like a lot of beer, but a half-barrel or keg holds around fifteen gallons, so that's only twenty kegs.

The aroma of caramel malt was strong, and I breathed in deeply as I went through the swinging door. Nicole was right behind me. She had been assisting me with brewing more and more lately. As much as I liked having the brewery to myself most of the time, I appreciated the help. And it was fun being on the teaching end for a change.

The next step in the process was to pump out the wort, which was the liquid formed from the mashed grain and water. Then we pumped it back into the brew kettle through a nozzle that forced the solids and hops to move into the center so when the tank was drained, the solids stayed. After that, we cooled the liquid quickly, added the yeast, and calculated the initial specific gravity. The initial gravity subtracted from the final gravity at the end of fermentation determined the ABV, or alcohol by volume—a very important number. By that time, it was the lunch hour, so Nicole returned to the pub while I finished transferring the stout to the fermentation tank. I set the temperature on the tank to sixty-eight degrees, where it would ferment for approximately two weeks.

My stomach was screaming for food by then, so I decided to get something to eat before I tackled the cleanup. Cleaning and sterilizing all the equipment took time, and I needed to be properly fortified first. Besides, I hadn't seen Jake yet this morning.

The thought of seeing my chef brought a smile to my face. I'd known Jake Lambert practically all my life. He'd been my brother Mike's best friend—and still was—and I'd had a crush on him for years. When my former chef, Kurt, had been murdered four months ago, Jake had walked back into my life. He'd just retired from playing professional hockey and happened to be a certified chef. One thing led to another and we were now what my mother called "an item."

I crossed the pine plank floor of the pub, stopping briefly to say hello to a few regulars. I liked that we had customers who kept coming back for the food as well as the beer. My stomach growled again as I went through the door to the kitchen. Two cooks plus Jake were in various stages of food preparation.

Jeannie Cross was assembling two grilled chicken salads and smiled when she noticed me. "Heads up, everyone. The boss is on deck."

"Uh-oh," Kevin Bruno said without glancing up from where he was sautéing some vegetables while simultaneously grilling burgers. "She must be hungry."

Jake was elbow deep in kneading some kind of dough. He looked up and winked at me. It never failed to make my stomach do that little flip and I felt my cheeks grow warm. "Either that, or she's here to fire your sorry behind," he said.

I laughed. I loved the camaraderie of my employees. They'd become my second family. "Don't worry, Kev. You're safe. As long as I get something to eat, that is."

Jake said, "Jeannie, fix Max one of those new turkey sandwiches we came up with." He held up his flour-covered arms. "I'd do it myself, but I'm a little indisposed."

"Coming right up." Jeannie put the finishing touch on the chicken salads by tossing a handful of French fries on top, which was a Pittsburgh tradition. I wasn't wild about it, but when customers kept asking for the fries, I gave in.

I followed her over to another stainless steel table, where she quickly assembled a sandwich on whole grain bread with roasted turkey slices, a thick slice of cheddar, baby spinach, and topped it with something that looked like a cranberry chutney or relish.

"Here you go, boss." She handed me the plate.

I took a bite. It was an interesting combination of flavors. The cheddar and turkey were familiar. The cranberry chutney was what made the sandwich. I tasted a hint of orange, and there was a little bit of heat to it also.

"Well?" Jeannie said.

"I like it. Especially the cranberries. I like the combination of sweet, tart, and heat." I swallowed the second bite. "I'm not sure about the spinach on here, though."

Jeannie looked smug. "That's what I told Jake."

Jake pushed the dough aside and went to the sink. "I guess I'm outnumbered—unless Kevin is going to back me up."

Kevin raised a hand. "I'm staying out of it. I don't even like cranberries."

I took my lunch to my office and finished the sandwich in record time, then buckled down to do some paperwork and make some calls. There was still a good bit that needed to be done for our Oktoberfest celebration. Jake had already come up with a special menu full of German food for that weekend—three kinds of wurst, schnitzel, sauerkraut, potato pancakes, and German potato salad. I made a note to pick up the menus at the print shop before the end of next week. I made a few phone calls, and after I updated my To Do list, I headed back to the brewery to clean up. A brewer's work is never done.

*T*he fire hall hosting the band I was hiring for our celebration was located just north of the city. Kristie drove, Candy rode shotgun, and Daisy and I white-knuckled it in the back. Kristie should have been a NASCAR driver. Thank goodness it was a short trip. I was tempted to make the Sign of the Cross when she screeched into the last empty parking space in the lot. I heard Daisy blow out air. She must have been holding her breath. Candy, however, didn't seem to be fazed one bit by Kristie's driving. Then again, I'd been a passenger in Candy's car. She drove as if the streets were an obstacle course.

The sound of accordion and horn music drifted across the lot when we got out of the car. "This is going to be so much fun," Candy said. Tonight she wore her best black and gold sequined blouse, black pants, and gold ballet flats. "It's been years since I heard this kind of music. It really takes me back."

"Back where?" I asked. I was constantly trying to get her to spill something about her background.

"To my much younger days." She turned to Daisy. "I'm so glad you decided to come with us."

Daisy smiled. "I am, too."

By this time we were at the door. Two women were seated

at a table with a steel cashbox and took our ten-dollar admission fees. There was a large sign welcoming us to their *Octoberfest*. I decided it wouldn't be polite to point out that they were a little early, or that they'd misspelled it by using a *C* instead of a *K*. It gave me a bad feeling about the beer they'd be serving.

The hall was decorated with black, red, and yellow streamers that matched the tiny German flags on every table. Not exactly the traditional Oktoberfest colors. Daisy caught my eye and made a face. I smiled at her and shrugged. At least they had the German part right.

Kristie pointed toward the far side of the hall. "There are some empty seats over there." We followed her across the room and sat at the end of a large banquet table. "I'm buying tonight," she hollered over the din. "What's everyone drinking?"

Daisy only wanted bottled water and Candy said she'd have the same. I offered to help Kristie and we headed to the bar. I was surprised at the assortment of beverages on hand, and especially that they had bottles of Oktoberfest beer from a local brewery. That moved them up a notch in my eyes. Despite the selection, Kristie and I also chose water for now.

It was too noisy in the hall for much conversation—especially with the band playing—so we sat and listened. The Deutschmen were very good, and hearing them play again made me glad I'd decided to hire them. The four musicians played accordion, trumpet, keyboard, and a sousaphone. I had to admit I'd never seen a sousaphone except in a marching band. I thought it an odd choice when a tuba would have worked just as well—or better. Plus it wouldn't have taken up half the stage.

There were only two couples on the dance floor until the band broke out in their version of the "Steeler Polka," which was sung to the tune of the "Pennsylvania Polka." A dozen people jumped to their feet, including Candy. She grabbed my hand. "Come on. You're dancing with me."

I tried to pull my hand back with no luck. "I don't know how to polka. I'm Irish. O'Haras don't polka."

"I won't hold that against you," she said. "It's easy. It's your basic one-two-three, one-two-three. Just follow me."

"Do I have any choice?" I asked as she practically dragged me across the room. Everyone in the hall seemed to know the words to the song, but I was too busy trying not to trip over my own feet to sing. By the time the song ended, I could reasonably say I knew how to polka, or at least fake my way through one. We stayed on the dance floor for the "Beer Barrel Polka," but I drew the line when the band began playing the "Chicken Dance." I had my pride after all.

I collapsed onto my folding chair and guzzled half of my water.

"Nice work," Kristie said with a grin.

"I can't keep up with her." I pointed to where Candy was enthusiastically flapping her arms to the music. "I don't know where she gets the energy."

"I don't, either," Daisy said.

The Deutschmen finished the song and announced they were taking a break and would be back shortly. A few minutes later, I went over to the bar, where the members of the quartet were quenching their thirst with cold beers. I'd only talked to one of them on the phone and had never met them in person, so I introduced myself. "Hi, I'm Max O'Hara."

The keyboard player shook my hand. "I'm Bruce Hoffman." He was in his mid to late fifties, with an obviously dyed crew cut that bordered on orange. He had a friendly smile that made up for his hair color faux pas. He introduced the others.

The trumpet player was Manny Levin, called "Toots" by his friends. Toots appeared to be in his sixties. He was bald and almost as wide as he was tall. The sousaphone player, Doodle Dowdy, was the youngest of the group—probably in his forties, with sandy hair that hadn't seen a barber in a while. The last member of the band, the accordion player, was Felix Holt. Felix appeared to be the oldest—close to seventy, or possibly even older. He had gray hair, gray eyes, and the deeply wrinkled skin of a smoker or former smoker.

I invited them over to our table, where we discussed my upcoming event and made the final arrangements. While we talked, I noticed Felix kept staring at Candy. Finally he said to her, "You look very familiar. Have we met before?" He spoke with a slight accent.

Candy shook her head. "Absolutely not."

"I never forget a face," he said. "Especially one as lovely as yours."

I expected Candy to roll her eyes and make some smart remark. The man was obviously flirting with her. Instead of a witty comeback she said, "You're mistaken."

"I don't think I am," Felix said. "I know you from some-where."

Daisy smiled at the man. "Maybe you've been to her bakery. It's the best one in Pittsburgh."

"Which bakery is that?" Felix asked.

"Cupcakes—"

Candy cut her off. "He's never been to my bakery."

"You're probably right. I'm sure I would remember the bakery," he said. "That's not it. I know you from somewhere else. I am sure of it. It will come to me."

"How many times do I have to tell you that you're mistaken? I don't know you and you certainly don't know me." She rose quickly to her feet. "I need some air. I'll be outside."

CHAPTER TWO

Daisy, Kristie, and I exchanged glances. What in the world had gotten into Candy? I'd never seen her treat anyone so rudely, unless they deserved it. Felix surely didn't.

"Excuse my friend," I said. "She's not usually like that."

"She's always the life of the party," Kristie added.

Doodle Dowdy took a swig of his beer. "Don't worry about it." He slapped Felix on the back. "He's always thinking he knows someone."

Felix had been staring at the door Candy had exited. "What did you say your friend's name was?"

I'd only used first names when I introduced everyone. "Candy. Candy Sczypinski."

He was silent for a moment then turned to his band mates. "I believe it's time for our second set, gentlemen." The others finished their drinks and followed him to the stage. As Felix adjusted the strap on his accordion, he glanced at the door one more time, then shook his head and launched into "Edelweiss."

Since my business was concluded, we headed outside to get Candy and head home.

I was at the brewery bright and early the next morning. By seven a.m. I'd already checked the fermentation tanks and inventoried the grain for my next order. Cupcakes N'at opened at seven, which was very timely because I was starving. Plus, I wanted to talk to Candy again and make sure she was all right. On the way home last night she'd explained that she'd just been tired after dancing two polkas. She hadn't meant to be rude to Felix Holt, but when he persisted with his notion that he'd met her before, she'd had enough. We'd teased her all the way home that Felix was only hoping to get lucky. She hadn't been amused.

Mary Louise and Candy were both at the counter and customers were lined up three deep when I entered the bakery. It was unusual for it to be so busy at this hour of the morning on a Saturday. But it was a beautiful day so everyone must have decided to get up and out instead of sleeping in. Candy was her usual cheerful self, talking and laughing with the customers.

"There's our Max," Candy said when I finally made it to the front of the line. "Can you believe the crowd this morning?"

"I hope you have a chocolate muffin left," I said.

"You're in luck," Mary Louise said. "We have two."

"I'll take both." I'd give one to Jake when he came in.

While Mary Louise bagged my purchase, I asked Candy how she was.

"Never better," she said. "It's amazing what a good night's sleep will do."

"I'm glad to hear it."

Mary Louise handed me the bag and I paid for the muffins. Customers were lining up again, so I bade them goodbye. I shouldn't have been worried about Candy. Everyone was entitled to be grumpy once in a while, and she was no exception.

Jake came in right after I got back to the brew house, so we sat at the oak bar in the pub to eat our breakfast.

"If you keep feeding me Candy's baked goods, I'm going to start looking like one of those muffins," Jake said after he'd practically inhaled his treat.

I reached over and poked him in the ribs. "Not likely." He wasn't losing his six-pack anytime soon. Although Jake didn't play professional hockey anymore, he still skated several mornings a week and played a pickup, no-checking game every chance he got. I'd gone skating with Jake a couple of times but I wasn't very good at it. He assured me I'd get better, but I doubted it. My exercise mostly consisted of walking to work when the weather was nice and hauling fifty-pound bags of malt up the steel stairs to the mash tun. Plus the touch football game every Sunday in my parents' backyard.

"How did it go last night?" Jake asked.

"We had a good time." I gave him all the details.

He grinned. "Sounds like that Felix guy was hitting on

Candy. That 'don't I know you from somewhere' line is one of the oldest in the book."

"He was certainly persistent." I gathered up our muffin papers, dropped them into the bag, and crumpled it up. "It would be nice for Candy to find someone. They seemed to be close to the same age and he seemed nice enough. Maybe I should try and do a little matchmaking."

"Do you think that's a good idea? If Candy got so annoyed with him that she walked out, she may not appreciate you butting in."

"I'm not butting in," I said. "Not really. Besides, Candy's always trying to fix everyone else up. Maybe it's time to give her a taste of her own medicine."

Jake slid off his stool and put his arms around me. "She didn't have to fix us up."

"No, she didn't. But she did try to convince me you were interested and I didn't believe her."

"She's a smart woman."

I laughed. "I'm going to tell her you said that."

"Uh-oh."

"Of course, I can be bribed into not squealing."

"Anything you want. It's yours."

I snuggled closer to him. "You can kiss me."

"You drive a hard bargain, O'Hara."

One of the servers called in sick just before lunch. It was too late to call someone else in, so I left Nicole in charge of the bar, donned an apron, and pitched in to help. It was a nice change of pace, even though on most days I stopped at various tables anyway to speak to the customers and thank them for choosing the Allegheny Brew House. The big difference today was making sure I got their orders straight. The brewery and manning the taps were my areas of expertise. Jake consulted with me with menu changes, but in the end I left the decision on what to serve to him. Cassie, my most experienced server, knew the menu better than I did and was quick to jump in when a diner had a question. Once again, I was thankful I had such wonderful employees. When the lunch rush was about over and only three tables were occupied, I grabbed a quick sandwich and took it back to my office.

I'd only swallowed the first bite when my cell phone rang. I didn't recognize the number so I didn't bother to answer it. A minute or so later my phone dinged that I had a voice mail. I finished my lunch before checking it. I didn't recognize the voice until the caller identified himself.

"Sorry to bother you, Miss O'Hara. This is Doodle Dowdy—one of the band members from last night."

I hoped it wasn't trouble and they were canceling on me. There would be no way I'd be able to find an adequate substitute at this late date. If at all.

"There's something very important I'd like to talk to you about. I don't want to discuss it over the phone, but if you would call me back as soon as possible, maybe we can make arrangements to meet somewhere." He left his number.

"What in the world was that all about?" I said aloud.

Nicole appeared in the doorway. "What was what all about?"

I told her about the message.

"Maybe he has the hots for you and that's his way to get you to call him," she said with a grin.

"Right."

Nicole rested a hip on the corner of my desk. "You don't think he's calling to cancel performing for our party, do you?"

I shook my head. "I don't think so. It didn't sound like it anyway."

One of the servers called Nicole's name and she stood. "Let me know what you find out. I'd hate for something to ruin our Oktoberfest."

I watched her leave, then picked up my phone and called the number Doodle had left. He answered on the second ring.

"Thanks for calling me back so quickly," he said.

"What can I do for you?" I asked.

"I need to talk to you. It's very important, and like I said in my message, I'd prefer to do it in person."

I bluntly asked him why. I didn't understand what it could possibly be that we had to meet in person.

He paused before answering. "It's kind of a delicate situation."

"Mr. Dowdy—"

"Call me Doodle."

"Doodle. I don't really know you very well." For all I knew, the guy was two pints short of a barrel. "I need to have some idea of what this is about."

"It has to do with what happened last night."

I began to relax. I understood now. I'd been right that Felix had been interested in Candy. He must have put Doodle up to making the call. This matchmaking thing was going to be easier than I thought. While trying to decide on where to meet, I discovered that Doodle owned a house in the Troy Hill neighborhood. My brother, Sean, was pastor of Most Holy Name of Jesus Church in Troy Hill, so I could go to Mass there in the morning (which would make Sean happy) then meet Doodle at his home. I hung up and pushed away from my desk wondering if I should surprise him and take Candy with me.

"**Y**ou can't go and meet him," Candy said later that day when I'd told her about Doodle's call. She had stopped for dinner on her way home after the bakery closed and we sat at a table in the corner of the pub.

"Why not?"

She put her fork down none too gently on her plate. "Because you don't know him. It's not safe. I would have thought you'd have more sense than that, what with your father being a cop and all. For all you know, that Doodle person could be a serial killer."

I couldn't help laughing. "I appreciate your concern, but he's harmless. He has something to tell me. That's all."

Candy leaned back in her seat and crossed her arms over her chest. "And just what could he possibly have to say that he couldn't tell you over the phone?"

I hadn't told her yet that I thought Felix Holt had put him up to it. "He said it was important." I paused. "I think it concerns you."

"Me." She uncrossed her arms and picked up her fork. "That's the most ridiculous thing I ever heard. He doesn't even know me." She picked at a piece of salmon on her plate. "I wouldn't fall for that if I were you."

"I think the accordion player put him up to it."

Candy's head snapped up from where her gaze had been focused on her plate. "The accordion player? Why in the world would you think that?"

"It makes sense to me. He seemed to be interested in you last night, and the fact that you wouldn't give him the time of day probably intrigued him even more. He figured this was the only way to find out about you. Why don't you come with me tomorrow and we'll see if I'm right?"

"No. Absolutely not."

"It might be fun," I said. "Don't you want to know what he wants to tell me?"

"No, I don't. I'm not going and that's it." She wagged a finger at me. "And I don't want you going, either."

We went back and forth like this a couple of times, and I finally gave up trying to convince her to come along. I left her to finish her dinner and went back to work. I couldn't get our conversation out of my mind while I drew drafts for customers. I didn't get it. Candy was being ridiculous. Why was she so dead set against me meeting with Doodle?

Doodle Dowdy's house was on a tiny side street only a block from Most Holy Name Church, so I left my car in the parking lot after Mass and hoofed it over. The Troy Hill neighborhood was like most of the older ones in Pittsburgh—the streets were narrow and the homes had been built close together. The home had red Insulbrick siding that had seen better days, but it looked like Doodle had attempted to do some updates to the rest of the house. The small front yard was enclosed with a shiny new chain-link fence. The front porch looked new as well—or at least freshly painted. A fiberglass front door had replaced what probably had been an old wood one. The door was open behind a new-looking full-view screen door.

There was no doorbell, so I knocked on the edge of the screen door. I waited a minute, then knocked again. Just then, there was a noise from inside the home. I called Doodle's name, and when there was no answer, I went in. "Doodle?"

His house was a shotgun style, where one room led to the next all the way to the back of the house. The living room where I entered was well lived in. There was a dark brown leather sofa with a matching recliner. The wood on the coffee table was scuffed, and several newspapers were scattered over the top. A large flat-screen TV just about filled one wall, and a narrow staircase led to the second floor.

The next room must have been a dining room at one time, but now was filled with empty canvases and paint supplies. There was a table pushed up against one wall that was littered with magazines, books, and what appeared to be sketchbooks. Evidently Doodle was interested in art as well as music. Odds and ends of assorted papers and sketches were strewn on the floor. There was an old upright piano on the other side of the room, and on the floor beside it there was a trombone and a plastic crate lying on its side with sheet music spilling out onto the floor. Doodle was not a very neat housekeeper.

From the next room, I heard a drawer open, then slam

shut and another one open. Doodle must be in the kitchen and hadn't heard me come in. I headed that way and pushed aside the curtain that was hanging in the doorway. With one foot barely in the room, I froze in place when I saw that the person making all the noise wasn't Doodle at all.

It was Candy.

CHAPTER THREE

"Candy," I said. "What are you doing here? Where's Doodle?"

She placed the papers she was holding onto the counter. "I have no idea where he is. I haven't seen him."

"What are you doing here?" I repeated. "I thought you didn't want to come."

"I changed my mind."

"You should have told me that before I got the surprise of my life finding you in the man's kitchen." It suddenly dawned on me what she had been doing. "Why are you looking through his stuff? And why isn't he here? We had an appointment."

"How am I supposed to know why he isn't here?" she

said. "Maybe he had to run to the store or something. He'll probably be right back, which means I need to stop yapping and go through the rest of these papers."

"Why?"

"I just do." Candy turned and opened another drawer. "I thought I told you not to come here today."

"You did. You also said you weren't coming, and you haven't explained why you're here."

"I told you I changed my mind." She opened and closed another drawer.

She wasn't making any sense. As a matter of fact, this whole scenario didn't make any sense. She had been adamant about not coming here with me and now she was nebnosing into Doodle's stuff. I grabbed her wrist and yanked it away from the drawer she was riffling through. "Stop. Right now. I want you to explain what the heck you're doing here, and don't give me that 'changed your mind' crap again. You're in someone's house without permission. You could be arrested for burglary—or least trespassing."

"Which means you could be, too."

"I'm supposed to be here." But she had a point. I should have waited on the porch for Doodle to return.

Candy touched my arm. "I'll tell you everything later," she said. "Right now, I have to find out what he knows before he gets back."

"Knows about what?"

Candy closed the last drawer and sighed. "There's nothing here. What am I going to do now?"

"I'll tell you what you're going to do." I took her by the

hand. "We're going to go outside and wait on the porch for Doodle and you're going to tell me what's going on."

She didn't argue with me. We went back through the dining and living rooms and took seats on the two plastic lawn chairs on the front porch. After what seemed like a long wait, although it was really only a few minutes, she said, "I guess I should at least try to explain."

"That would be nice."

"I thought I'd get here before you had a chance to talk to Doodle to find out what he wanted to tell you."

"Isn't it obvious?" I said. "He wants to fix you up with Felix Holt."

Candy sighed. "Oh, Max. You have a good heart. The best heart of anyone I know, but I'm sure that's not why he wanted to see you."

"No?" What else could it be?

"I have a feeling he's fishing for information, and not because Felix Holt is interested in me. At least not interested in the way you're thinking."

"I don't understand."

"The truth is, Felix—" Her phone rang and she reached into the pocket of her slacks. "I'm sorry, but I have to get this." She got up and walked to the other end of the porch.

I couldn't hear any of her side of the conversation other than "I'm glad you called" and "I'll be waiting."

When she finished the call, she pocketed the phone and turned back to me. "I'm sorry, but we'll have to finish this later. I have to go."

"What about talking to Doodle?"

"It's going to have to wait. You'll have to fill me in on what he tells you and don't tell him anything about me. Not yet. Not until I know what's going on. As far as he's concerned, I was never here."

Dumbfounded, I watched her walk down the street and get into her car. I was so confused. She'd gone from not wanting me to talk to Doodle at all, to wanting me to tell her everything he said. Candy was definitely going to have some explaining to do.

I waited on Doodle's porch for another thirty minutes but he didn't show up. The longer I waited, the more annoyed I became at both Doodle and Candy. I finally took a slow walk back to my car in the church parking lot, still trying to figure out what was going on. I was at a total loss. None of it made any sense. None at all.

W hen I got back to my apartment, I poured a bowl of cereal and sat down at my kitchen counter with it. Hops, my gray tabby, jumped onto the counter as I poured the milk. "Sorry, kitty," I said. "This is my breakfast. You already had yours."

She butted her head against my hand as I lifted a spoonful of cereal. Milk splashed onto the counter and Hops proceeded to lap it up. I laughed. "You did that on purpose, didn't you?"

"Murp." She had a very self-satisfied look on her face.

I rubbed the top of her head. There was nothing like a kitten to calm a person down. By the time I finished my cereal, I felt a little more normal. But I was still annoyed—especially at

Candy. "What was she doing?" I said aloud. "And why did she leave in such a rush?"

Hops tilted her head. She obviously didn't know, either. Not that I expected her to actually answer, but she was a good listener. And it was better than talking to myself.

I set my bowl in the sink, then picked up the cat and put her on the floor. I had several hours before I had to be at my parents' house for Sunday dinner. Jake wasn't picking me up until one so I had plenty of time to try and figure out what exactly was going on. I grabbed my cell phone and parked myself on the sofa.

The first thing I did was listen again to Doodle Dowdy's voice mail that he'd left for me yesterday. I was glad I hadn't deleted it yet. His message said, *There's something very important I'd like to talk to you about. I don't want to discuss it over the phone, but if you would call me back as soon as possible, maybe we can make arrangements to meet somewhere.* He hadn't mentioned either Candy or his friend Felix at all. But when I called him back yesterday, I remembered he had told me it had to do with "what happened last night." Had I misunderstood? He hadn't come right out and said he wanted to fix Felix up with Candy. I had assumed that's what he wanted. Maybe Candy was right after all.

That didn't explain what she'd been doing in Doodle's house, however. She had to have had a good reason to be rooting through his stuff. I trusted Candy and I knew she'd tell me eventually. I just wasn't all that patient and didn't like waiting. In the meantime I'd try and get ahold of Doodle and find out why he wasn't home this morning.

I called the same number I had the day before and his

voice mail picked up. I left a message that I was sorry I'd missed him somehow that morning and if he still wanted to meet, to let me know.

When Jake picked me up—along with Hops in her carrier—I told him about what happened that morning. He was as puzzled as I was about Candy's behavior. "She's usually so straightforward about things. It's definitely not like her," he said.

"I know."

"She said she'd tell you though, right?"

"Yeah. I just don't like waiting. My curiosity is killing me."

Jake laughed. "Forget about it for now and think about how my team is going to beat your team in this afternoon's game."

We played touch football with family and neighbors just about every Sunday in my parents' backyard. Along with Sunday dinner, it had been a ritual for as long as I can remember. Dad was a detective with the Pittsburgh Bureau of Police, and on the Sundays he got called out, we played without him. With five older brothers, I was something of a tomboy and had enjoyed playing as much as they had. I remember once when I was about ten years old, my brother Joey made the mistake of telling me football wasn't for girls and I should be in the kitchen with Mom. Suffice it to say, he never told me that again. At the moment, I was on my brother Mike's team and we usually won, but Jake's team had beaten us the last two Sundays in a row. Mike and I had already discussed strategy over the phone, though, and we expected to go back to our winning ways. "Not a chance, Lambert," I said. "You're going back to being a loser."

"Ouch. That hurts."

I leaned over and kissed his cheek. "Just on the football field, of course. You'll always be a winner in my heart."

"That's much better," he said. "But you're still going to lose today."

It turned out that he was wrong. The next-door neighbors who usually played with us were away for the weekend, but fortunately we were able to round up some new players. Philip Rittenhouse and Marcus Crawford had recently moved into the house across the street, and it didn't take much convincing to have them join in. Philip and his partner were on opposite ends of the spectrum as far as appearances went. Marcus was bulky and muscular with sandy hair and brown eyes. His skin was deeply tanned. Philip, on the other hand, was tall and slim, and he didn't look like he spent much time outdoors. His eyes were a bright blue and his hair was prematurely gray. If I had to guess their ages, I would say they were in their early forties.

Philip played on Jake's team with Dad, and Mike and I took Marcus under our wing. Mike was thrilled to find out that Marcus had played college ball.

"Nice game," Jake said afterward when we moved to the patio. "I didn't know you'd have a ringer on your team, though."

"I didn't know, either," I said. "Honest." I began pouring a round of beer from a growler filled with the last of my summer citrus ale. I was going to miss this beer, but it was almost fall and time for a heartier brew.

"Sure you didn't," Jake said.

Mike plopped into the seat beside him. "All's fair in love and football."

Jake laughed. "Just wait until next week."

"Don't count on it, loser," Mike said with a grin.

"Maybe Marc and I should switch teams next time," Philip said, taking the glass of beer I handed to him.

"Now that would be fair," Jake said.

I finished passing out the beer. "He has a point, you know."

Mike said, "You're only saying that because he's your boyfriend. What happened to family loyalty?"

I grinned. "Actually, I'm saying that because Jake needs all the help he can get."

That got a big laugh out of everyone. I headed inside to help Mom and my sister-in-law Kate finish dinner preparations, and check on Hops. I found her in the living room sitting contentedly on the lap of my niece, Fiona, who had just turned three years old a week ago and liked to make sure everyone knew it. They were on the sofa beside Fiona's older sister, Maire, who would be five in December. Maire was reading to them from a picture book. I told them dinner was almost ready. Hops's ears perked up at the word *dinner*, and she jumped down and followed me back to the kitchen. I fed her and she curled up on her blanket in the spot she had declared was hers in the corner of the kitchen.

Since they were new to the neighborhood, my mother had invited Philip and Marcus to join us for dinner. My brother Sean, the pastor, had left for his annual Labor Day retreat after Mass that morning so he wouldn't be joining us. Since it was a holiday weekend, Mom went all out with picnic-type food—coleslaw, baked beans, and ham barbecue made with Isaly's chipped ham, of course—a Pittsburgh staple. Kate brought a strawberry pretzel salad for dessert. Dinner was set up buffet style, so we all fixed a plate and headed back outside.

Jake and Mike were already talking sports with Marcus, so I took the seat in between my mom and Philip. Kate sat across from us with the two girls. I asked Philip how he liked the neighborhood so far.

He smiled and his eyes crinkled at the corners. "I love it. It's a wonderful place. It's not all that different from Brooklyn, where I used to live. A little less hectic is all. Your parents have been so nice to us."

"We're happy to have you in the neighborhood," Mom said, then to me, "Philip is the new owner of Gallery on Ellsworth in Shadyside."

"That's an art gallery, right?" I asked, feeling kind of stupid that I didn't know.

"Yes," Philip said. "I worked in a major gallery in Manhattan for ten years but was in the market for a place of my own. There's a lot of competition there and I couldn't find anything that was affordable for me. When this gallery came up, Marcus and I discussed it and decided it was perfect. We were both ready for something new, and here we are."

I smiled. "Welcome to Pittsburgh. I'll have to stop by your gallery soon."

"Maybe we can fix you up with some art for your brew-pub," Philip said.

I couldn't imagine anything I'd find in an art gallery would fit with the pub décor. Besides, one wall had a large window to show off the brewery and the other wall was brick. There were always the restrooms, but I didn't think Philip would appreciate that. I probably couldn't afford anything he sold anyway. "What kind of art do you sell?"

He wiped barbecue sauce from his hands with a napkin. "Anything and everything at the moment, although I'm trying to pare down our selection to bring in some more serious pieces. Museum-quality pieces. That's what we dealt in where I worked before. I just facilitated a purchase for a client I met in New York that I'm very excited about. It's a Vermeer."

The name sounded vaguely familiar and I tried to place it.

Mom said, "I take it it's not *Girl with a Pearl Earring.*"

Now I knew who it was.

Philip chuckled. "Not exactly. The one I'm acquiring is one of several of Vermeer's works that appeared on lists several centuries ago, but never surfaced. They were all assumed to be lost. The fact that three of them have turned up recently is astounding."

I asked him what the painting was like.

"It's one of Vermeer's early works, only known as *Face by Vermeer.* From what I've learned, it was most likely painted around 1660, several years before the famous *Pearl Earring.* As a matter of fact, *Pearl Earring* is believed by experts to be modeled after this painting. The subject in this painting is just as lovely."

Dad had been trying to keep track of both the sports and the art conversations, but now moved his chair closer to ours. "How did the seller manage to obtain paintings that had been lost for that long?"

"So far I only know that they came from an old estate in Austria that was in the process of being demolished," Philip replied.

"Austria?" Mom said. "Wasn't Vermeer Dutch? Austria's a far cry from Holland."

"It's possible the paintings had been in Nazi Germany and somehow made their way into Austria. No one really knows at this point," Philip said.

"How do you know it's really a Vermeer?" Dad asked. "Have you met the seller?"

Philip shook his head. "I haven't met him, which isn't unusual in this business—it's more the norm. Our contact has been via e-mail since he lives out of the country. The painting was delivered by courier and I wired the funds to his bank after I received documents that verified the authenticity. He had lists of the experts he used in the process, including tests that were done on the painting. It seems to be the real deal."

"You said there are three paintings?" I said.

Philip nodded. "According to the seller, the other two are in the process of being vetted. Once they're authenticated, he plans to put them up for sale as well."

"It sounds like you're being thorough," Dad said.

"I am," Philip said. "The buyer wants to take possession of it as soon as possible, but I'm still double-checking everything the seller gives me. And there is additional independent testing being done as well. It's too large and too important of an acquisition not to take the greatest care."

"I don't mean to be rude," I said, "but shouldn't paintings that important go to museums?"

"Technically, yes," Philip said with a smile. "The seller apparently offered them to several, but they couldn't pay the price he's asking. With budget cuts, many museums don't have the funding for acquisitions like that. Some have generous donors, so maybe eventually the paintings will end up on display somewhere. They shouldn't be locked away where no one can see them. My client has agreed to let me display the painting for a short time, so I'm happy about that."

The rest of the evening passed quickly. It was filled with interesting conversation ranging from Philip's gallery and how Marcus went from being a linebacker in college to bank vice president, to the brew house and Dad's police stories. By the time Jake dropped me and Hops off at home, I was exhausted.

I got the kitten settled, then got ready for bed myself. I was just about to turn out the light when I remembered the battery on my cell phone was low and thought I'd better plug it in and let it charge overnight. I slipped out of bed and went back to the kitchen, where I'd left my purse on the counter.

I was surprised to see the voice mail notification on my phone. I hadn't heard it ring, but then again my purse had been inside the house all day. The message was from Doodle. "I'm sorry I missed you earlier. It's a long story and I still want to talk to you. There's a hall where we practice sometimes down on the North Side. If you can get away, I'll be there tomorrow night at eight." He left directions to the rehearsal hall. I called back and left a message that I would see him then. Maybe now I'd finally find out what he wanted to tell me.

CHAPTER FOUR

When I went next door to Cupcakes N'at on Monday morning, Mary Louise was manning the counter by herself. There was a line of customers halfway to the door, but she was very efficient and kept them moving. It wasn't long before it was my turn.

"Where's Candy?" I asked after we'd exchanged greetings and I ordered a cinnamon raisin bagel.

"She took the day off," she said. "Can you believe it?"

I didn't remember Candy ever taking a day off. "Is she sick?"

Mary Louise shook her head. "She said she just had some things to take care of today. She was here most of the night baking and she left right after I got in at six."

I wondered if it had something to do with the phone call

she received yesterday when we were at Doodle's house. "She didn't tell you what she had to do?"

"No, and I didn't ask. She caught me by surprise—especially since today is a holiday. It must be something pretty important for her to leave the bakery in anyone else's hands." She smiled. "I'm flattered that she thought I could handle it."

"Why wouldn't she?" I took the bakery bag she passed to me and paid her for the bagel. "You know what you're doing and Candy realizes that."

"I appreciate that," she said. "Maybe now she'll take a day for herself a little more often. It would do her good."

I told Mary Louise to call the brew house if she needed anything. I didn't think she would, though. Candy had left the bakery in very capable hands for the day.

I headed across the street to Jump, Jive & Java for an iced mocha. It looked as if all of Lawrenceville had the same idea. Kristie and two other baristas worked feverishly behind the counter serving up everyone's favorites. Most customers were taking theirs to go, so when I finally got my mocha, I took it to my favorite table beside the *Casablanca* poster, where I sat and listened to some guy singing about accentuating the positive. I was almost finished with my bagel and drink before it slowed down enough for Kristie to join me.

"Whew," she said, plopping down into the chair across from me. "I didn't expect it to be this busy on Labor Day. Isn't everyone supposed to be going to picnics?"

"I guess they had to get their caffeine first."

"Apparently." Kristie took a long drink of her iced green

tea. "Did you see that Candy took the day off? I went over earlier before it got busy here and Mary Louise said she wouldn't be in." She shook her head. "Frankly, it's about time she did that. I sure don't plan on working seven days a week when I'm her age."

I shrugged. "I can't imagine ever retiring. If it's something you love to do, why not keep doing it?"

"True. Which means I'll be lying on a beach somewhere in the Caribbean when I hit retirement age."

"With anyone in particular?"

"Wouldn't you like to know." Kristie grinned. "My love life is none of your business, and if I recall correctly, you told me the same thing more than once when I tried to find out what was going on between you and Jake."

"Touché." I drained my mocha and tried again. "Is it someone I know?"

"Maybe. Maybe not." Kristie finished her drink and stood. Customers were lining up again.

"Not even a hint?"

She shook her head.

"A tiny one?"

"Forget it." Kristie laughed and headed back to the counter. "Besides, I kind of like keeping you in suspense."

I had to get back to work, too, so I said good-bye and crossed the street to the brew house.

I wasn't brewing today, so after I checked the tanks and did some cleaning up, I went back to my office. I worked on the payroll and the server schedule. Ordinarily, I'd make calls to suppliers on a Monday, but because of the holiday, that task would have to be postponed until tomorrow. After a while, my mind wandered to the upcoming meeting with Doodle, and that made me think about Candy. She had promised to tell me why she'd been at his house, but so far I hadn't heard a word from her. I had hoped to see her this morning and get some kind of explanation before tonight. Her taking the day off nixed that. Or maybe not.

I picked up the phone and pressed her number on my speed dial. I almost hung up when I got her voice mail then decided to leave a message. I told her I was meeting Doodle tonight but didn't give any details. Now she'd have to call me back if she wanted to know more.

The day passed quickly even though we weren't extremely busy. There was a steady flow of customers for growler refills, and some even bought extras of the half-gallon jugs to be sure they had enough beer for their Labor Day picnics. The restaurant also kept up a steady pace although there were a few empty tables throughout the afternoon.

I still hadn't heard from Candy by the time Nicole came in to relieve me at six. Jake was leaving the kitchen in Jeannie's capable hands since I'd talked him into coming with me to see Doodle. We had plenty of time before the meeting, so I headed home to feed Hops. Jake would pick me up there.

I had only walked two blocks when my phone buzzed. It was Candy. "I was wondering when you were going to call me back," I said.

"I've been busy. I had a lot to do today," she said. "I thought we'd settled this business of you meeting with Doodle."

I didn't know where she'd gotten that idea. This whole

thing was far from settled. "He still wants to talk to me. Don't you want to know what he has to say?"

"Yes, I do. That's why I'm going to meet you there."

"Why don't you ride with Jake and me? Your place is on the way. It won't be any trouble at all to pick you up."

"Thanks, but I have a few more things to do. I'll just meet you there."

I had a sneaking suspicion she was planning to show up before we got there, just like she had on Sunday morning. I didn't want a repeat of that. Doodle and I had agreed on eight o'clock, so I told Candy we were meeting him at eight fifteen. I reluctantly gave her the address and said we'd see her there. I pocketed my phone and walked the remaining few blocks home.

After I fed Hops and changed clothes, the kitten seemed to know I was going out again. She jumped and attached herself by her claws to the khaki shorts I'd changed into. I carefully peeled her off and placed her on her favorite blanket on the sofa. "Sorry, kitty. But I won't be long."

She gave me her version of the evil eye. She didn't believe me.

Feeling guilty, I grabbed her treats from the kitchen counter and put a few on her blanket. "I'll give you more when I get back."

She gobbled them up, circled twice, and settled down. I scratched the top of her head and went out to meet Jake.

The rehearsal hall was in a partially renovated building on the North Side's East Ohio Street. This area had once been thriving and had gone through a major downturn over the years but now seemed to be on its way back up. East Ohio Street was lined with an eclectic mix of mom-and-pop shops and bars, a restaurant or two, a pawn shop, and a photography museum. There was a major hospital only a block away, and the street was within walking distance to the North Shore area and Heinz Field, where the Steelers played football, and PNC Park, the home of the Pirates. My good friend, Dave Shipley, had a brewpub nearby. I hadn't talked to him lately and realized I should give him a call before the next brewer's association meeting at the end of the month. Dave had been a big help when Jake and I were trying to figure out who killed the nasty food critic Reginald Mobley.

Jake parked his truck in a small lot on a side street and we walked the three blocks to the address Doodle had given me. The building looked like it had originally been a bank or something equally impressive. It was three stories tall and built of massive granite blocks. Large windows were almost a full story tall. The modern door made of glass and stainless steel didn't fit the building and I wondered what the original had looked like. A heavy mahogany door would be my guess.

It was a quarter to eight and Candy hadn't arrived yet so we waited on the sidewalk in front of the building. When she rounded the corner five minutes later, I caught a flash of surprise on her face. I was right—she had planned on getting here first.

"How was your day off?" I asked.

"Busy," she said. "I ran a few errands, things like that. Mary Louise handled everything at the bakery just fine."

Jake said, "You should do that more often. It'll do you good."

"What will do me good is to go inside and find out what this Doodle person has to say." She reached for the door.

Jake and I exchanged looks. It wasn't like Candy to be short like that. Especially to Jake. I put my hand on the door. "Wait."

"Why?" she said. "We're not that early."

"That's not it." I searched for the right words. "You haven't been yourself since Friday night at the fire hall when Felix Holt thought he recognized you. Then there was yesterday morning at Doodle's house. I'd like to know what's going on with you."

Jake squeezed her shoulder. "We're your friends. You shouldn't hesitate to tell us anything."

Candy looked at me, then Jake, then back at me and sighed. "You're right. After we talk to this Doodle character, we'll go someplace and I'll tell you what I can."

Jake opened and held the door that Doodle had said he'd leave unlocked. The lobby of the building had been gutted and the walls partially reconstructed. Drop cloths covered sections of the marble floor, and the rest was covered with dust from workers hanging and sanding the drywall. Doodle had told me the rehearsal space was on the second floor so we headed toward a staircase on the far side of the building. Although Doodle hadn't said any of the other band members would be here, I half expected to hear music. Instead it was eerily quiet.

The stairs were of the same marble as the floor and my sneakers made little squeaky noises as we went up. The hallway on the second floor looked like something out of an old movie. The oak doors that lined the corridor had large frosted glass windows with numbers painted on them. Some had names on them. I wouldn't have been the least bit surprised if one had been lettered *Sam Spade, Private Eye.* "This is so cool," I whispered.

"Why are you whispering?" Candy asked.

"I don't know. It's just so quiet in here."

"I doubt that it's very quiet once that band starts up," Jake said. "This is really a weird place for a rehearsal hall."

"Maybe it's only temporary," I said. "Once the renovation is done, I imagine they'll try and fill all these offices. A rehearsal hall doesn't really fit. Can you imagine trying to work in an office with someone playing a sousaphone down the hall?"

"Or even worse," Jake said. "How about a heavy metal band?"

Candy said, "They might be able to soundproof it."

"Good point," Jake said.

"Would they want to go to that expense, though?" I said. "I'd think the owner would make a bigger profit leasing office space. Most bands probably couldn't afford the monthly rent."

By this time we'd reached the end of the hall. Doodle had said it was the last door on the left. The oak door had the same kind of glass as the others and had the number *212* painted on it. Jake turned the knob and pushed it open.

The room was much bigger than I'd expected. Half the room was open space with a dozen or so metal folding chairs scattered about. The other half was divided by partition-type walls as if it had been an office not too long ago. Nothing here had been renovated yet. The plaster walls were cracked and there were spots where the plaster had completely fallen off the wall. There was still gridwork for a suspended ceiling hanging above but all the panels were missing. Bare light-bulbs hung from the original high ceiling. I didn't see any musical instruments anywhere, but I guessed no one would want to leave them lying around. I didn't see Doodle any-where, either.

"Doodle?" I called. He didn't answer. The three of us crossed the scuffed wooden floor toward the partitions.

"I don't think he's here," Jake said.

"Maybe he's just late." I hoped he hadn't stood me up again.

"Then why was the door unlocked?" Candy said.

We started looking behind partitions. Other than more folding chairs and a couple of music stands, they were empty. Candy was a little ahead of us, and when she reached the last cubicle, she stopped. "Oh no."

"What is it?" I asked.

She put her hand up. "Stay there, Max."

It was too late. I had already reached her, and Jake was only a step behind me. I stopped beside Candy in the door-way. It looked like we'd found Doodle.

CHAPTER FIVE

Sheet music was scattered across the floor, but that wasn't the worst of it. Doodle was lying among it, with most of his head stuffed into his sousaphone. Candy leaned down and felt his neck for a pulse. She straightened and shook her head. An image of my friend Kurt flashed in my mind, and the dinner I'd eaten before I left the brew house threatened to come up. I turned away and took a deep breath.

Jake already had his phone out and I heard him talking to the 911 operator. When he finished, he put his arm around me. "They'll be here in a few minutes. Let's wait out in the hallway."

I leaned into Jake for comfort. "I can't believe it. Poor Doodle." It wasn't right for anyone to end up like that.

Candy paced back and forth. "I should have known some-thing like this would happen."

"How could you?" I said. "You didn't even know the man."

She seemed more agitated than upset. "No, but—" She was interrupted by the sound of pounding footsteps on the stairs.

Two uniformed officers appeared and one stayed in the hallway with us while the other one entered the room and made sure Doodle Dowdy had truly departed this earth. The next hour was a blur of activity. We were made to wait downstairs while more police and crime scene techs and detectives arrived.

The three of us were separated to get our statements. I was thankful that it was my dad's day off. I didn't want to have to deal with Dad or his partner, Vincent Falk, at the moment. The detective who caught the call was Mitch Raines. He was a good friend of my dad's so I was sure Dad would get the full account anyway. Mitch's partner took Candy aside and another detective took Jake.

I got Mitch, who joined me on the stairs. He dusted off the step with his hand before sitting beside me. I wasn't sure why he bothered cleaning it off. Considering how he was dressed, it was kind of pointless. He wore old ratty jeans and was unshaven. Either he was working undercover on something or he'd just rolled out of bed. He was one of the detectives on the Allegheny County District Attorney's Drug Task Force, so it could be either one of those or a combina-tion of both.

"Was the victim a friend of yours?" he asked.

"No, I barely knew him." My voice was shaky. I'd seen

more than my share of dead bodies over the last six months. You'd think I'd have gotten used to it, but I hadn't. The realization that Doodle had been murdered was shockingly real.

Mitch squeezed my arm. "Take your time. Just tell me what happened."

I told him about hiring the band for Oktoberfest and how Doodle had called me and said he had something to tell me. I told him about going to Doodle's house on Sunday and how he hadn't shown up. I didn't mention that I'd found Candy there. I knew I should tell him, but I didn't want to get her in trouble. I'd leave it up to her to fill them in on that score.

"Do you know what Doodle . . . That's an odd name, isn't it?"

"His real name was Walter," I said. "But the other band members called him Doodle. He even referred to himself by that nickname."

Mitch nodded. "Do you know what he wanted to tell you?"

I shook my head. "Not really. I thought it was because one of the other band members seemed interested in Candy over there." I pointed across the room. "I figured we could fix them up."

Mitch smiled. "Playing matchmaker?"

"Sort of. She's always trying to fix everyone else up so it would have served her right."

"What made you think that's why the deceased wanted to see you?"

"It's the only thing I could think of. Doodle mentioned

that he wanted to talk to me about what happened on Friday night. You see, when we went to see the band on Friday night, the accordion player kept trying to talk to Candy, saying he knew her from somewhere."

"One of the oldest lines in the book," Mitch said.

"That's what Jake said, too. And when Doodle told me he wanted to talk to me, fixing them up was the first thing that came to mind. As a matter of fact, it was the only thing that came to mind. I can't imagine what else he could have wanted to tell me."

"Maybe he was interested in you," Mitch said. "And the friend thing was just a reason to see you."

I shook my head. "I don't think so. He never gave me that impression."

"You mentioned that the victim belonged to a band. Can you give me the names of the other band members?"

"Sure. Felix Holt—he's the one who was talking to Candy—Manny Levin, and Bruce Hoffman. I have their information if you want it." I took my phone from my pocket and pulled up a contact. "This is Bruce Hoffman's number. He's the one I talked to about hiring them."

Mitch had written down the names as I rattled them off and he did the same with the phone number. "Did it seem like they got along? Was there any tension among them?"

"I didn't notice anything unusual, but I really didn't know them. I'd only met them the one time at the fire hall on Friday night."

He asked if I'd noticed anything unusual when we arrived tonight or any suspicious activity in the neighborhood. I told him I hadn't. After a few more questions Mitch said I could go and if I thought of anything else, to let him know.

I got up and crossed to where Jake was standing by the door. He pulled me into his arms and kissed my forehead. "Are you all right?" he asked.

"I will be." I looked around. "Where's Candy?"

"She's waiting outside for us. She had to make a phone call."

When we reached the sidewalk, however, Candy was nowhere to be seen.

I tossed and turned all night. I couldn't get the image of Doodle with his head stuck in his sousaphone out of my mind. And then there was Candy. I alternated between being mad at her and worrying about her. Something was terribly wrong and I couldn't figure out what it was. I had been so annoyed with her on the way home that Jake had really gotten an earful. I was pretty sure he learned a few German swear words before he dropped me off at my apartment. I finally gave up on sleeping at four a.m. I played with Hops for a while and fed her before I got showered and dressed. I was at the brew house by five thirty, and the first thing I did was go into the kitchen to make a pot of strong coffee. Once the caffeine kicked in, I headed into the brewery.

One of the brown ales was ready for kegging so I figured I may as well get that out of the way since I was here so early. I readied the sterilized stainless steel half-barrel kegs and moved them over to the tank. I connected the fill tube to the tank and the first keg, then attached a tube with a valve to the top of the keg. As it filled and the CO_2 in the keg was gassed off, I got the next one ready. When the valve started releasing foam and then beer, it was full. It was a nice, mindless task, and when I was done, I felt a lot better.

Jake came in just as I finished cleaning up. "Looks like I missed all the fun." He kissed me on the cheek and looked around. "You kegged all these this morning? What time did you get here?"

"Around five thirty. But I was up at four. I couldn't sleep. I couldn't stop thinking about last night."

He put his arm around me and we walked through the pub to the kitchen. "I didn't sleep that great either so I went to the rink and skated. There was a high school hockey team practicing and I gave them some pointers."

I smiled. "You must have loved that." He'd never come out and said so, but I knew he missed playing hockey. He still skated every chance he got even though he couldn't play professionally anymore.

"It was fun." He grinned and his brown eyes lit up. "I even got to autograph a few sticks." He opened the refrigerator and got out eggs and cheddar cheese.

"What are you doing with those?" I asked.

"Making you breakfast, what else?"

"That's the best offer I've had all week."

He grinned again. "I aim to please, ma'am."

After Jake and I ate breakfast, he started prepping for lunch and I took a walk next door to Cupcakes N'at. I half expected Candy to have taken another day off just to avoid me, but she was behind the counter by herself, waiting on a handful of customers. She was cheerful as ever to the customers, but she looked like she hadn't gotten much sleep, either. She caught my eye and waved.

I waited until everyone had been served. When the bakery was finally empty, she apologized for leaving so suddenly last night.

"I'm sure you had a good reason," I said, hoping she really did. "I'm worried about you, though. You haven't been yourself since Friday night." When she opened her mouth to protest, I said, "Don't try to deny it. There's something wrong and I want to help."

"I know you do." She glanced at the door as another customer came in. "And I know we need to talk. I'll be here late tonight to get caught up on some things. Can you stop over around nine or so?"

I agreed and went back to the brew house. I had fifteen minutes before we opened for the day, so I thought this might be a good time to make a phone call or two. I sat down at my desk and called Bruce Hoffman. He picked up on the second ring. After I identified myself, I offered my condolences.

"Thank you, Max," he said. "It's such a shock to all of us."

"It was to me as well."

"I don't know why Doodle was even at the rehearsal hall. I told the detective that we didn't have a rehearsal scheduled last night. We played at a party earlier in the day and I assumed everyone went home after that."

"I don't know if the police told you this, but I was supposed to meet Doodle at the rehearsal hall last night and I was the one who found him."

"No, he never mentioned that. Thank goodness you didn't arrive earlier. You might have been attacked, too."

"Maybe if we'd gotten there earlier, Doodle wouldn't have been killed."

"We?"

"I had friends with me."

"The same friends as the other night?"

"Only one of them, and my boyfriend." I always felt strange using the word *boyfriend*, but I didn't have a substitute for it.

"If you don't mind me asking, why were you meeting with Doodle anyway?"

I shifted in my seat. "I really don't know why he wanted to see me. He didn't want to discuss whatever it was over the phone. He wanted to do it in person."

"He didn't give you any idea?" Bruce asked. "Not even a hint?"

"Not really. I was kind of hoping you might have some idea what he wanted."

"I wish I could help you," he said. He paused. "If he wouldn't tell you what he wanted, it couldn't be very important. I wouldn't worry about it if I were you." Before I had a chance to ask him if he thought it could be about Felix thinking he recognized Candy, I heard his phone beep.

"I have to go," he said. "I have another call coming in. Thanks for calling. And don't worry—we still plan on playing for your party."

I pressed the End Call button but he'd already disconnected. It was just as well. He seemed to be as much in the dark as to what Doodle had wanted as I was. He certainly was curious to know, though. Maybe he'd call me if he figured it out. I didn't have time to think about it any further. It was time to open for the day, so I headed out to the pub.

The lunch rush was over, and since the pub was empty for the moment, I was polishing the bar top. I looked up when I heard the door open. It was my dad. That could only mean one thing.

He kissed me on the cheek and slid onto a bar stool. "Mitch called me."

"I figured he would." I folded the polishing cloth and placed it under the bar.

"Are you all right?" he asked. "You should have called me."

"I'm okay." I didn't address the not calling him part because I knew he was right. "Can I get you something to eat or drink?"

"Just some water." Dad rested his elbows on the bar. "Tell me what happened. Mitch said you were supposed to meet with the victim. Who was this person?"

I filled a glass with ice and water and placed it in front of him. "He's—was—a member of the band I hired for Oktoberfest." I told him about going to see the band on Friday night and that Doodle had called twice and wanted to talk to me but didn't want to do it over the phone. "I only agreed because I thought it was about Candy."

"Why would you think it was about Candy? Did he know her?" Dad asked.

"No, but Felix Holt, one of the other band members, thought he recognized her from somewhere. Candy denied it but I thought maybe Felix was interested in her and that he had put Doodle up to it."

"But he never mentioned any of that over the phone?"

"Not in so many words."

I tried to think of a way to bring up the fact that the first time I went to meet Doodle, Candy had been at his house. I knew if I told Dad, she'd immediately be a "person of interest," even though she was a friend and she'd been with Jake and me when we found Doodle.

Dad was quiet for a minute, then he said, "You're not telling me something."

I didn't have to find a way to tell him after all. I should have known he'd see it on my face like he always did. I'd never make a living playing poker. "I don't want you getting all bent out of shape about it. It's really nothing."

"Why don't you let me be the judge of that?"

I hoped he wouldn't be judge, jury, and executioner. "The first time I was supposed to meet with Doodle, Candy was there."

"Did she go with you?"

"Not exactly."

"Not exactly." There was a touch of sarcasm in his voice.

"You're not going to like it," I said. "When I got to the house, Candy was already there."

"What do you mean by that? She was waiting outside for you?"

I almost said "Not exactly" again but thought better of it. "She was inside Doodle's house."

"Mitch didn't mention that."

"That's because he didn't know. I thought it would be better if Candy told him, so I didn't say anything."

"Maybe you'd better start at the beginning. And don't leave anything out this time."

So I filled him in, giving him all the details of our night out to see the band perform, Candy looking for something at Doodle's house, and the three of us finding Doodle's body. I didn't specifically mention Candy's odd behavior lately, but I didn't have to. It was fairly obvious. When I'd finished, Dad pulled his cell phone from his pocket. "What are you doing?" I asked.

"Calling Mitch. You're going to have some explaining to do, young lady."

"Why didn't you tell me all this last night?" Mitch Raines asked. He'd arrived twenty minutes after Dad called him, and the three of us were sitting in my office.

"I didn't want to just blurt it out and get Candy in trouble. I thought it best to leave it up to her to tell you. Besides, she was with Jake and me when we found Doodle. There's no way she had anything to do with it."

Mitch sighed. "That's not the point. You may be right that your friend didn't have anything to do with the murder, but she should have told us everything. And you should have, too."

I knew he was right but I still hated that telling him could get Candy in trouble.

"Tell me again the chain of events—when you arrived, when Ms. Sczypinski arrived."

I told him Jake and I got there around seven forty-five and Candy arrived not long after that.

"Is there a chance Ms. Sczypinski arrived before you, then doubled back and met up with you?" Mitch asked.

"No way." I shook my head. "Absolutely not."

"I know Ms. Sczypinski is your friend, but sometimes we don't know our friends as well as we think we do. You said yourself that she wanted to talk to the victim. She was upset. She got angry. Maybe she didn't mean to kill him—"

"No! Absolutely not! Candy did not kill Doodle. She wouldn't hurt a fly, let alone another human being."

Dad had been silent so far, but now he spoke up. "Then she won't mind talking to the detectives again."

"Of course she won't," I said. I felt like I should be crossing my fingers behind my back. "Just because she was in Doodle's house doesn't mean she had anything to do with his murder. I'm sure she'll be happy to clear this up."

Mitch stood. "You could be right that she had nothing to do with it, but you know we have to look into everything, Max. We can't just assume someone didn't commit a crime. This whole thing could be as simple as a burglary gone wrong. We just don't know yet. Not until we have all the facts."

I appreciated the fact that Mitch wasn't trying to railroad anyone, unlike what Vincent Falk had tried to do back in

July when he was sure Jake and I had committed murder. He'd been my dad's new partner at the time and was a little too intent on making a name for himself. We'd called a somewhat uneasy truce since then.

Dad stood, too. "Don't worry, sweetie. It will all work out."

"I hope you're right."

As soon as they left, I picked up the phone and dialed the bakery. Candy must have been busy because the voice mail picked up. I left a message. "Detective Raines will be getting in touch with you. It's a long story, but my dad knew I was holding something back and I ended up telling them about you being at Doodle's house." I paused, wondering what else I could say. "I'll talk to you tonight."

But for now I had to get back to work.

CHAPTER SIX

The late afternoon and dinner hours were busy. From what I could gather from going table to table and drawing drafts at the bar, no one felt like cooking the day after a holiday. I was thrilled—it was great for business. Things were winding down a bit around seven, so I was taking the opportunity to stack some clean pint glasses behind the bar when I heard a familiar voice.

"It's nice to see someone in this neighborhood is working."

"Hi, Elmer," I said.

Elmer Fairbanks was ninety-two years old and still going strong. To say he was colorful would be an understatement. He was very opinionated and never hesitated to let anyone know what he was thinking. I'd met him through the library book club that Candy and Kristie also belonged to. Somehow he'd become part of the group. At least we always knew his book choice would have something to do with the Old West or World War Two. He wore his 101st Airborne ball cap today instead of his Stetson, which meant he was in a feisty mood. When he wore the Stetson, he was more likely to be the laid-back cowboy sort. He definitely wore the ball cap more often.

Elmer slid onto a bar stool. "I want to know what's going on, young lady. And don't argue with me and give me any of this 'I don't know what you're talking about' crap."

An argument was exactly what he wanted. He loved verbally sparring with anyone and everyone, so I obliged. "But I don't know. Can you be a little more specific?"

"For a smart girl, you act kind of dumb sometimes."

"Is that meant to be a compliment? If it is—"

"Oh, for heaven's sake." He slapped a five-dollar bill down on the bar. "Pour me one of those lagers and I'll spell it out for you." He took a long drink after I placed the beer in front of him. "Ahh." He wiped his mouth with the back of his hand. "Just like the ones we had after we crossed the border into Germany back in forty-five. Best beer in the world."

"Now that's definitely a compliment. Thank you."

"Did I ever tell you about the time me and the boys raided the beer and wine cellar of some Kraut muckety-muck?"

He had. More than once. "I think so," I said. "But you can tell me again."

"You just want me to change the subject, don't you?"

I smiled. "I wasn't the one who changed the subject."

"Don't get smart with me or I'll tell your mother."

He had a twinkle in his eye so I knew he was enjoying the verbal sparring. I was, too.

Elmer pushed his glass to the side and leaned on the bar top. "What was that cop doing here before? I was over in the coffee shop and I saw your pop come in, which is no surprise. I figured he was just visiting. Then that other detective showed up. What gives?"

"How did you know that was a detective?"

"I didn't fall off the turnip truck yesterday, you know. I can spot a gumshoe a mile away."

"So, what do you want to know?"

"Everything. And while you're at it, why wasn't Candy at the bakery yesterday? Mary Louise didn't have my donut with extra jimmies set aside."

"I didn't know Candy did that for you. With all your bickering, I didn't even think you liked each other."

"Just because we like to argue only means we like to argue," he said. "Now quit beating around the bush and fill me in."

I began with the party at the fire hall on Friday night and ended with my discussion with Detective Raines. I had to pause once to fill a growler for a customer, and a couple of times to draw drafts.

"You've had a busy weekend," Elmer said when I'd finished. "What's the plan?"

"I don't have one, other than talking to Candy."

"Want to know what I think?"

Even if I didn't, I knew he'd tell me anyway. "Sure."

"That Howdy Doody character—"

"Doodle. His name was Doodle."

Elmer shook his head. "What the heck kind of name is that for a grown man? Anyway, Doodle knew something about that Felix fellow that he wanted you to know. And I think it's pretty strange that Candy was afraid of what he knew."

"I don't think she's afraid," I said.

"Maybe not, but she sure as shooting wants to know what he knew. We have to find out exactly what it was. And mark my words, she's met that Felix fellow before; otherwise she wouldn't care what Howdy Doody had to say."

I didn't correct the name again and agreed with him that Candy knew Felix from somewhere. "Candy promised to tell me everything."

"That's a start," Elmer said. "While you talk to her, I'll ask my buddies at the VFW what they know about that band. I'm pretty sure they played a party or two there."

I was glad he didn't want to come with me to see Candy. That wouldn't have gone over well at all. Instead of Candy telling me what was going on, she and Elmer would be at each other's throats and I wouldn't learn anything at all. He promised to get back to me as soon as he had any news.

Elmer wasn't gone for five minutes when Daisy walked in. "I just talked to Kristie." She hopped up onto a bar stool. "What the heck is going on? She told me one of the band members was killed. She saw something on the news and recognized the name. The reporter said he was murdered by a possible intruder."

"Did they say anything else?" I asked.

"Like what?" Before I could answer, her eyes grew wide. "You didn't. Tell me you didn't find another body."

I felt my face get warm. "I wish I could tell you that."

Daisy grabbed both of my hands. "Oh, Max. How horrible for you. I'm so sorry. What happened?"

I wished I could have gathered everyone else I knew together and only have to tell the story once more. I'd lost count of how many times I had repeated it. It was getting monotonous. "Do you remember how the one band member thought he recognized Candy on Friday night?"

"Was he the one who was killed?"

I shook my head and explained everything that had happened since then. "I'm worried about Candy," I said when I'd finished.

"I was so busy on Saturday that I didn't see her, and then I was closed Sunday and yesterday. Now I feel bad that I didn't check on her."

"You shouldn't feel bad," I said. "You didn't know anything was going on."

"That's not the point. I've spent too much time focused on my own issues without even thinking about anyone else's problems."

"You had good reason to take care of yourself."

"I know I did, but that's over and done with now. I'm starting over. I've put that horrible man out of my mind for good. I'm not going to let one bad person ruin my life," she said. "What can I do to help?"

I didn't have to think about it for long. My friends—and especially Candy—had banded together to help me on more than one occasion. The least I could do was to do the same for Candy. Back when I was trying to figure out who killed my friend and assistant, Kurt, she had given our little group a ridiculous nickname, but now I was going to use it again. "What are you doing tomorrow evening?"

"Not a thing," Daisy answered.

I grinned at her. "If Kristie and Elmer are free as well, I propose another meeting of Max's Marauders."

Daisy returned my grin and gave me a high five. "I'll be there."

"I thought you didn't like that name," Jake said. We had just wrapped it up for the day and were leaving the brew house to go next door to the bakery. The pub was in Nicole's capable hands for the rest of the night and I was filling Jake in on what he'd missed over the last couple of hours.

"I didn't at the time, but Max's Marauders seems to fit. Besides, Candy was the one who came up with the name. She'll like that we're using it again."

He put his arm around me. "It does kind of have a nice ring to it."

Since Cupcakes N'at was closed for the day, we had gone through the pub kitchen saying good night to the remaining kitchen staff, then out the door to the alley that ran behind the businesses. The alley was wider than some in the city—wide enough for garbage trucks to enter to empty the Dumpsters behind the stores. And for the occasional fire truck. I had learned that firsthand when the person who killed Kurt set a Dumpster on fire to try and scare me away. The bakery had a steel fire door just like the one at the brewpub. As a matter of fact, the only difference between it and any of the places that opened onto the alley was that mine also had a garage door that opened into our storage area. It made it convenient for deliveries like large bags of hops and malt.

I pounded on the bakery door with my fist. "Candy, it's me and Jake." Seconds later the door opened.

"Come on in," she said.

As soon as we were through the door, Candy pulled me into a bear hug. Jake took a step backward, probably to avoid the same fate.

"I'm sorry I put you through so much this weekend," she said.

I extricated myself from her arms. "Did you get my message about Detective Raines?"

"Yes, I did," she said. "I'm meeting with him tomorrow morning. I didn't mean to put you in that situation."

"I know you didn't, but you do owe me an explanation."

Candy sank onto a stool beside a stainless steel table. "I didn't kill that man."

"I know you didn't." I took a seat on the other side of the table and Jake followed suit.

There was a long pause as she tapped her Steelers-decaled fingernails on the table. "I'm not sure where to start."

Jake said, "The beginning usually works."

She looked from me to Jake and back again. "I'll tell you what I can, but there are some things that I can't talk about."

"Why not?" My concern was beginning to turn to aggravation. I wanted to know everything.

"It's complicated," she said. "It involves a lot of people,

and my former employer would frown on me talking about certain issues."

I'd wondered numerous times about Candy's background. She often knew what was going on before anyone else did. She had a knack for being able to find out anything about anybody. At first I thought she was just a gossip, but as I got to know her better, I realized there was a lot more to it. Anytime I asked her about how she knew so much, she changed the subject or gave me a dumb reason to explain how she came about certain information. I wasn't going to accept her excuses this time. "I don't care what your former employer wants. You don't work for them anymore. You don't owe them anything."

"Maybe. Maybe not." She stopped tapping her nails and folded her hands on top of the table. "I don't want to put anyone else in danger. The less you know the better."

"You're not making any sense."

Candy sighed. "Like I said, it's complicated."

I wanted to pull the information out of her. As hard as it was, I kept quiet and waited. I learned from my dad that if you were quiet long enough, the other person became uncomfortable with the silence and tried to fill it. He'd gotten a lot of confessions from people that way. Including one from me when I stayed out way past curfew when I was sixteen. I should have known it wouldn't work on Candy, though. When I stared at her, she stared right back. I finally caved. "So explain it to us."

"I've always liked to bake. When I retired, all I wanted to do was own a bakery and make irresistible treats to make people happy. I made good money over the years and I had enough saved to buy this place and not have to worry about being in debt. It was something I'd looked forward to for a long time. It was a change to a very different career."

Jake smiled. "That sounds familiar."

Candy patted his hand. "You know what I'm talking about, then. I had almost forgotten you made a drastic change of your own."

Going from playing professional hockey to being a chef was definitely a career change.

"Anyway," Candy said, "I thought I'd left my old life behind me. I thought I'd be safe."

I didn't understand. "Safe? From what?"

A timer dinged. "I have to tend to this batch."

While Candy went to the oven and removed several trays of thumbprint cookies, I impatiently tapped my foot on the floor until Jake touched my arm. "That's not going to accomplish anything," he whispered. "Be patient. Let her tell her story in her own time. We're not going anywhere."

"What if Mitch Raines decides not to wait to talk to her tomorrow and hauls her off to jail instead?"

"Then she'll have all the time in the world to talk to you."

"You're a lot of help."

He grinned. "You're welcome."

Candy loaded up the oven again and sat back down. "Where were we?"

"You mentioned something about thinking you'd be safe," Jake said.

"I've kept this to myself for so long I'm not even sure how to explain. I know you've had questions for a long time about what kind of work I used to do, Max."

"How did you know that? I never said anything out loud."

Candy smiled. "You didn't have to, dear. You dropped plenty of hints and your curiosity was written all over your face."

"Speaking of curiosity," I said, "What exactly did you do before?"

Candy looked at Jake. "She's not very patient, is she?"

"No, she's not." He squeezed my hand.

She took a deep breath before continuing. "I worked for the government."

I wasn't exactly surprised. "Why is that such a big secret?" I asked. "I've met a few feds before and they didn't hesitate to say where they worked."

"I'm sure they must have been with other agencies—not the one I worked for." Candy folded her hands on the top of the table and stared at them. I was about ready to reach over and pull the rest of the story out of her when she finally said, "I worked for the CIA."

I'd long suspected something to that effect, but it felt strange to hear it from her own lips. It explained how she knew background on a lot of people and how she seemed to know everything that went on, sometimes before things happened. "The CIA?"

Jake added, "You were a spy?"

"I guess you could call it that," she said. "Although at the agency we referred to our jobs by other names."

"I'm sorry," Jake said, shaking his head. "But I just can't picture you as a spy. You're more like someone's grandma, not some Mata Hari."

"You never saw me in my younger days," she said with a smile.

I'd seen a few photos of Candy when I'd been to her house, but I hadn't paid a whole lot of attention to them. When I asked about them, all she said was that she'd spent some time in Europe when she got out of college. I remembered one had the Roman Coliseum in the background and one had the Eiffel Tower in Paris. She'd been "quite a looker," as Elmer would have said, with her long blond hair and miniskirt. And her clothes weren't all black and gold then, either.

As much as I wanted to hear all about her former career, it wouldn't explain anything that had happened over the last few days, and that was why we were here. We could delve into the past later. "Why were you at Doodle's house on Sunday?"

"To find out what he knew." Her tone of voice made it sound like she should have added "duh" to the end of the sentence.

"About what?"

"Felix Holt."

It suddenly hit me how ludicrous it had been that I had thought Felix was romantically interested in Candy. Maybe it was the stress of the whole situation but I started laughing.

Candy gave me a stern look. "I'm glad you find this so amusing."

Still laughing, I said, "I'm sorry. I was just thinking about how when all this started, I thought you were avoiding Felix because he wanted to get into your pants."

"What?" Candy's eyes widened. I'd never seen her look so shocked.

I shrugged. "It made sense at the time."

Jake tried to suppress a laugh with no luck. "Max was going to try and fix the two of you up."

She shook her finger at us. "This situation is nothing to laugh at. Felix Holt—"

Just then there was a knock on the door.

"Shh." Candy put the finger she'd been shaking to her lips.

The knock continued in something that sounded like it might be a code.

Candy seemed relieved. She relaxed. "It's okay." She got up and opened the door. A man who looked to be in his early seventies came into the room.

Dapper was the first word that came to mind as I took in his appearance. He was very old-time British, right down to the white curled mustache and bowler hat. He even carried an umbrella. He removed his hat and bowed when he spotted me and Jake.

Candy kissed him on the cheek. "Thanks for coming." She turned back to us. "Max and Jake, I'd like you to meet my husband, Tommy Fleming."

CHAPTER SEVEN

My jaw just about dropped to the floor. I couldn't have heard her right. "Husband?" Candy was married? My mind couldn't wrap around that thought. When did this happen? How did this happen? Where did she meet him? Why had she never said anything?

"If you want to get technical," Candy said, "he's my ex-husband."

"Ex-husband," I said. I was beginning to sound like a parrot.

Tommy grinned and put his arm around Candy. "I think she's a bit flummoxed, my dear."

"Of course she is, but she'll get over it." Candy motioned for Tommy to sit. "Would you like a cup of tea?"

"That would be splendid, if it's not too much trouble."

He took a seat across from Jake, and the men shook hands. "You must be this young lady's beau."

Jake introduced himself and they chatted while Candy went about boiling water for tea and removing trays from the oven like having her secret ex-husband show up was an everyday occurrence. I couldn't do anything but stare at Tommy. I was still at a loss for words, which didn't happen all that often.

Tommy reached across the table and patted my hand. "I'm sure you have a lot of questions. We'll have some nice tea and some of Candace's lovely biscuits and we'll have a little chat."

Candace. He called her Candace. Other than some of the names Elmer had used, I'd never heard her called anything except Candy.

"*Maxine* is such a beautiful name," he said. "Perfect for a beautiful young lady."

I finally snapped out of it. Staring at the man was not going to answer any of my one thousand and one questions. I thanked him for the compliment, then said, "Will one of you please tell us what's going on? Candy, why didn't you tell me you're married?"

"Was married." Candy reached for a box of Earl Grey on a shelf then turned to Tommy. "I told you she was impatient."

"I've been very patient," I said. "Thanks to me, the police haven't knocked down your door and hauled you off to jail."

"The police are the least of our worries, my dear," Tommy said.

"Candy should be worried about the police. She's not in

the clear yet. Detective Raines was not happy when he found out she'd been in Doodle's house," I said. "Did she tell you what happened?"

Tommy nodded. "Candace told me everything."

"Here you go." Candy set a plate of cookies on the table. "I made your favorite."

Tommy picked up a snickerdoodle and bit into it. "I've missed these, love."

I cleared my throat. "I don't mean to be rude, but do you think you could have your little reunion later? We have more important things to discuss."

Candy brought a teapot and four cups to the table. "Fine." She sat down beside Tommy and poured. "Remember the other night when Felix Holt was sure he knew me?" she said to me.

"How could I forget? He wouldn't take no for an answer."

"The truth is . . . he was right. He did recognize me."

"Then why did you deny it?" Jake asked. "What was the big deal?"

Candy glanced at Tommy, and he patted her hand. "Go ahead and tell them, love. They need to know what we're dealing with."

"I had to pretend I didn't know Felix Holt," she said. "I had no choice. Until I know why he's here, it's better that he doesn't know who I am. Frankly, I was shocked that he recognized me after all this time. I don't exactly look the same and I haven't seen him since 1968."

"But he does know who you are," I said. "We told him your name. He even knows you own this bakery."

"He doesn't know Candace by her real name," Tommy said. "She went by another moniker back then."

"I take it he wasn't an old boyfriend," Jake said.

Tommy chuckled and Candy made a face. "Hardly," she said. She slid the plate of cookies across the table. "It's a long story. You're going to need these."

Finally. We were going to learn the truth. I leaned forward and rested my elbows on the table.

Candy took a sip of tea then said, "When I was about to graduate from Georgetown—"

"You went to Georgetown?" I blurted out.

Candy gave me the look she usually reserved for Elmer. "Are you going to interrupt me every sentence? If so, I'm going to stop now."

"Sorry," I said. "I'll shut up."

She continued. "I was in my last year at Georgetown in 1966. I was twenty-one years old, with a major in European studies and a minor in political science, and I was ready to take on the world."

I opened my mouth to ask how she went from that line of study to baking cookies, then quickly closed it again. I had no doubt she'd end her tale if I so much as let out a peep.

"A few months before graduation, there was a career expo with a lot of local companies and, since we were in the DC area, many government agencies. I hadn't had much luck with my job search up until then. I'd go on an interview and the boss would basically pat me on the head and offer me a secretarial job."

I couldn't imagine anyone trying that now. Or even Candy putting up with it.

"I wanted more than that," she went on. "It wasn't long before I realized no one had any use for a woman with a

European studies degree. The career expo was my last chance to find a meaningful job. If I didn't, I'd have to move back to Polish Hill and live with my parents, and I sure didn't want to do that."

Candy picked up the teapot and refreshed our tea. I reached for another cookie to go with it. I could see why these were Tommy's favorites.

She looked at me and Jake. "You're too young to remember this, but '66 was the year after U.S. troops were deployed in Vietnam. Protests were minimal at this point, but a lot of my classmates didn't want to have anything to do with the government. I was arguing with myself whether or not I should talk to any of the government recruiters when one of them got up and came over to me. He asked me if I wanted to make a difference in the world. I said I did, and as soon as I graduated, I had a job with the CIA."

Candy was silent so I figured it was safe to talk now. Except I didn't know what to say. Thankfully, Jake did.

"Just like that they hired you?" he asked.

She was more patient with Jake than she was with me. She even smiled at him. "Not exactly. I lost count of how many interviews and tests I took. The training was intense. Even with my degree, I didn't know as much about Europe and the Soviet Union as I thought I did. Over a year's time, I had to learn the ins and outs of the politics of the area, including learning several languages."

"What about the rest, like all the spy stuff?" I imagined a young Candy running around like a female James Bond.

"The spy stuff, as you call it, was part of that training."

"I still don't understand why you've kept this all to yourself over the years," I said. "It's not like you would have revealed anything top secret. And what does any of this have to do with Felix Holt or Doodle Dowdy?"

"We're getting to that." Candy rested a hand on her ex-husband's arm. "Maybe you should tell this next part, Tommy."

"Certainly." He drained his cup and pushed it aside. "When Candace finished her training, she was sent across the pond to the U.K. I was with British Intelligence and we routinely worked with the Americans. I was assigned to be her mentor. I was not in the least bit thrilled with the idea of babysitting a fledgling recruit, especially some flighty female. We hadn't yet been introduced, so I decided to play a little prank on her. I picked the lock on her hotel room door while she was out. When she returned and entered the room, I grabbed her from behind. Within seconds, I was flat on my back with her foot on my throat." He smiled and his eyes twinkled. "That was the last time I thought of Candace as a flighty female. I'm fortunate she didn't hurt me too badly."

I laughed, picturing the whole scene. It was such an incredible story. I couldn't believe Candy had kept it to herself for so long. "What happened next?"

"We became good friends and eventually fell in love," he said. "When Candace was sent to Czechoslovakia—"

"Czechoslovakia?" I said.

Candy gave me the look again.

Tommy continued. "I was already in the country when Candace was sent to join me in 1968." He picked up another cookie and took a bite. "What do you know about what is called 'Prague Spring'?"

I wished I had paid more attention in my history classes. I tried to remember anything I'd learned about that era. The only thing I could recall was that the Vietnam War had been going on during those years. I couldn't remember anything else. "Absolutely nothing," I said. "I've never heard of it."

"I'm not familiar with it, either," Jake said.

"Consider this your history lesson then," Tommy said. "In 1968, the Cold War was still in full force. The leader of the Communist Party in Czechoslovakia at the time was a man named Novotny. In the spring of that year, he was replaced by Alexander Dubček. Dubček instituted quite a few reforms in the country—almost a democratization of sorts. This didn't sit well with those in power in the Soviet Union. In August, the Soviets and the other Warsaw Pact countries invaded Czechoslovakia. Dubček was removed from power and taken to Moscow. All of his reforms were invalidated."

"How were you and Candy involved in all this?" I asked.

Candy picked up the story. "Tommy had been working with an underground organization and helping to facilitate some of the changes that Dubček was implementing. Although there was wide support from the general public, there were also a lot of hard-core Communists attempting to sabotage any efforts to bring about a democracy. I arrived in Prague in June."

She got a faraway look in her eyes. "It was the most beautiful city I'd ever seen. The places in Europe I'd visited up till then had lost many of their historic buildings during

World War Two. Prague had escaped much of the destruction. Centuries-old buildings stood like they'd be there forever."

"It sounds romantic," I said.

Candy took Tommy's hand and squeezed it. "It was."

Tommy said, "It was also a dangerous place. It wasn't always apparent who your friends were."

"Is this where Felix Holt comes in?" Jake asked.

"Yes," Tommy replied.

Candy picked up the narrative again. "Just like I had used an alias back then, so did Felix Holt. His name was Josef Bartek and he worked in Dubček's cabinet. What we didn't know was that the KGB had placed him there to keep an eye on Dubček and report anything that was contrary to the Communist way of thinking. He was very good at his job, and we had no idea he wasn't on our side. Maybe we should have suspected he wasn't when he was kept in place after Dubček was removed from office. Josef told us that he had convinced them that he'd been working against Dubček all along. And he continued to feed us little bits of information. It was a long time before we figured out he only gave us what they wanted us to know."

"In other words," Tommy said, "he knew all about our underground efforts while we knew nothing about him. By the time we noticed the bug he'd planted in our flat when we'd had him over for dinner, it was too late. Many members of the group we'd been working with suddenly disappeared. We began to hear about raids and mass arrests. We finally came to the conclusion that our good friend Josef was behind it all."

Candy stood. "I'm going to put some more water on for tea."

"Thank you, love," Tommy said. He smiled at me. "I know this is quite a bit to take in."

He wasn't kidding. It was like hearing a movie plot. "You two have led such exciting lives."

Candy sat back down. "It was our job. We were only doing what we'd been hired to do."

Jake said, "Yeah, but most people aren't hired to be spies."

I was anxious to get back to their tale. "What happened next?"

"We didn't want to believe that someone we thought was our friend had betrayed us," Tommy said. "We set a trap of sorts to see if we were correct that Josef had been working against us."

"We fed Josef some false information," Candy said. "We took advantage of the bug in our flat. We invented a new leader of the democracy underground and even invented a plot to overthrow the current government. We made sure to mention that there would be a meeting at a certain place at a certain time." The kettle whistled and she got up again.

While Candy fixed the tea, Tommy continued the tale. "KGB agents ended up raiding the empty building where the supposed meeting was to take place. After that, Josef had to have known we were on to him, so we planned on leaving Prague."

"Why didn't you just capture Josef?" I asked.

"Because we still needed information from him," he said. "Other agents were to take our place and try to build a relationship with him."

Candy returned with the teapot and filled our cups. "Unfortunately, that never happened."

"Why not?" Jake asked.

Tommy sipped his tea before answering. "We'd already vacated our flat and had been moved to a house on the outskirts of the city. We were to catch a flight back to London that night, but somehow Josef found us as we were about to leave the house."

This was definitely sounding like a movie plot.

"When we opened the door," Tommy said, "Josef stood there holding a gun."

"Oh, no." My heart beat faster, picturing this in my head.

Tommy went on. "I was unarmed and he forced us back inside. He ranted like a madman about how we had betrayed him. I looked for a way to make a move and try to disarm him. At one point during his rant he raised the gun to the ceiling and I began to move toward him. He saw me and lowered his weapon. I thought it was the end for me." He took Candy's hand in his.

"Don't stop there," Jake said. "What happened?"

Candy's face was pale when she answered. "I shot him. I shot Josef Bartek."

CHAPTER EIGHT

I couldn't quite believe what I'd just heard. Silence hung in the air for what seemed like a full minute although I'm sure it wasn't that long. "I thought you were unarmed," I said when I found my voice.

"Tommy was," Candy said. "My purse was hanging on my shoulder and my gun was in it. Tommy was in front of me blocking Josef's view, so I was able to slip it out unnoticed."

"We heard sirens then," Tommy said. "We had to leave immediately. I had to pull Candace from the house. We didn't know whether Josef was dead or alive, but it was too dangerous to stay. If we had been arrested for shooting a government official . . ."

He didn't need to finish the sentence to spell out what would have happened.

Candy's hand shook as she lifted the teapot. She noticed that our cups were still full and set the pot down again. "It's something that's haunted me all these years—thinking that maybe I had killed someone."

Tommy put his arm around Candy's shoulders. "You had no choice, my dear."

"I know that. It didn't make it any easier." She looked across the table at Jake and me. "It was the one and only time I had to fire my weapon. I'm sorry you had to hear all this. Now you see why I didn't want to talk about any of it, or what I used to do. It's better left in the past."

I reached across the table and took Candy's hand. "I'm glad you told us."

"I am, too," Jake said. "Especially now that Josef or Felix or whatever his real name is, has turned up here."

"Why do you think he's in Pittsburgh?" I asked.

"That is what we need to discover," Tommy said. "Until we know, Candace is in grave danger."

The four of us had talked until almost midnight. When I asked Candy and Tommy to join us at Jump, Jive & Java for the meeting of Max's Marauders, she was thrilled that I'd decided to use the name that she had come up with. She said they'd try to make it, depending on how her meeting with Mitch Raines went. Although Mitch would probably reprimand her for rummaging through Doodle's house, he had no reason to hold her for anything—especially once she told him what she'd told us last night.

Despite the late night, I was up and at the brewery at my usual time. After I checked the tanks, I crossed the street to the coffee shop to see Kristie. The shop wasn't too busy, and when it was my turn, I ordered a caramel macchiato for a change and asked Kristie if she had a minute.

"Sure." She fixed my macchiato, poured herself a plain coffee, and told her assistant she was taking a break.

We sat at our usual table under Bogart and Bergman and I couldn't help but think of Candy and Tommy. A different era of course, but still. "Jake and I talked to Candy last night," I began, then told her the whole story.

"Wow," Kristie said when I'd finished. "I never imagined anything like that. I figured maybe she'd been with the FBI or something, but never thought she was a real, honest-to-goodness spy. And she was married! She never even said a word about that. Did she tell you why they broke up?"

I shook my head. "It wasn't a good time to ask. I think they still really care for each other. You should have seen the way they looked at each other, and Tommy kept calling her 'love.' It was very sweet."

Kristie leaned back in her seat and sipped her java. "Have you told Daisy or Elmer yet?"

"Not yet. I'll give Daisy a call after she opens up. If Elmer comes in this morning, maybe you could fill him in."

Kristie made a face. "He's not going to like being the last to know."

"He'll just have to get over it." I finished my drink and

stood. "We need to come up with a plan. Is it okay if we all meet here tonight? There's more privacy here than in the pub."

"You don't even have to ask. How does eight o'clock sound?"

"Perfect."

Jake wasn't in yet when I got back to the pub, so I went back to my office to do my daily paperwork. I updated the accounts receivable and payroll, all the while thinking about the strange events of the last few days. I still couldn't quite get over Candy's revelation. And the more I thought about it, the more I was convinced that Doodle's murder was somehow connected to Felix. It couldn't be a coincidence. Somehow he had to have discovered the connection between Felix and Candy, and that's what he'd wanted to tell me. The big question was how—and from whom. Had Felix found out Doodle knew his secret? And if he had, that made Felix the prime suspect in Doodle's murder.

When I came out of my office at ten, I almost bumped into Fran Donovan, who had just opened the door to go down to the cellar. Fran was a local historian who was working on adding a brewing museum downstairs. Her father had been employed by the Steel City Brewing Company from before Prohibition to sometime in the seventies. She had been instrumental in discovering the tunnels that ran under several businesses in the area, including the brew house. When we first met, we'd been at odds. She hadn't wanted my business here, but when she realized I wasn't trying to destroy her brewing heritage, she came around. When I suggested she add her museum downstairs, we even became friends.

Fran jumped about a mile when I opened my door, which was saying something because she was shorter than I was. She reminded me of a tiny mouse.

"I'm sorry," I said. "I didn't mean to startle you."

Fran put her hand to her heart. "That's quite all right. I should have realized you'd be in your office." She reached up and pushed her wire-rimmed glasses up her nose. "I hope you don't mind. I carried some boxes down earlier and I thought I'd get a few more things in order—especially if we plan to open the museum in time for Oktoberfest."

"I don't mind at all," I said. "Do you need any help?"

She shook her head. "I don't, but I'd love to show you a few things if you have time."

I said I did and followed her down the steep stairs to the basement. My pulse still quickened when I thought about the killer who had cornered me down there several months ago. The person who had killed my friend and assistant, Kurt, had known how some of the businesses were connected underground. He'd wanted my building for himself and was willing to commit murder to get it. When he trapped me in the cellar, he had marched me to the river, where he'd planned to get rid of me. Permanently. Since then I'd added more lighting than was probably necessary and had the concrete block walls painted a nice calm cream color. Its current appearance was nothing like before. It still looked like a cellar, but at least it was a nice bright one. Eventually I'd have the space redone and finished, and use the room as a rathskeller, which is the German word for a beer hall in a cellar. It would be great for special events and for the overflow from the pub that I hoped to have. In the meantime, Jake and Mike had made some rustic benches, which we'd put around the perimeter. They'd come in handy for seating for when Fran's brewing museum opened.

Fran led me through the door to the cavernous area where she was setting up her museum. Out of habit, I glanced toward the passageways that had been open a mere four months ago. Another change I'd made was to have doors installed with double deadbolts. I wouldn't be opening them again anytime soon. Maybe never.

Fortunately, Fran had done wonders with this space. What had been a dark and dank brick-walled cavern had been transformed into a light and bright space worthy to house the brewing history of Pittsburgh. The redbrick walls and domed ceiling had been thoroughly cleaned. She had contractors come in and tile the cracked cement floor, install LED spotlights, and hang strings of globe lights from the ceiling—all on her own dime. I had offered, but she refused to take any money from me. She said it was her way to honor her father's legacy.

"Here's what I wanted to show you." She opened a display case that held about a dozen or so photographs and lifted one out. "I just found this one last week."

I took the photo from her. She had captioned it *The Blessing of the Barrels*. In the photo, a priest in long black garb held an aspergillum, which was a perforated metal ball on the end of a stick used to sprinkle holy water. His arm was raised over a half-dozen wooden beer barrels. But that wasn't the best part. The priest and the barrels were on the sidewalk in front of Most Holy Name—the very church where Sean was pastor. I smiled at Fran. "Where in the world did you find this?"

Fran's eyes twinkled behind her glasses. "I knew you'd get a kick out of that one. I found it in an antique store. There was a bin of old photos. I like to go through those bins whenever I see them even though I don't usually find anything. But I did this time. Isn't it great?"

"I love it," I said. "Can I get a copy to show Sean?"

"I have something even better." She reached into one of the cardboard boxes on the floor and pulled out a wrapped package. "This is a little gift for you."

I tore open the brown paper. Inside was a framed eight by ten enlargement of the photo. I started to tear up. "You didn't have to do this."

"Yes, I did," she said. "You've done so much for me— letting me put my museum down here. It was the least I could do."

"If anything, I'm the one who owes you," I said. "If it hadn't been for you, I never would have known any of this existed." I smiled again. "Plus, I accused you of murder once. I definitely owe you."

"Well, I didn't have very nice things to say to you, either. Let's just call it even."

"Agreed." We chatted for another minute or two and she showed me some of the other displays she'd been working on. I couldn't wait for the public to have a look at some of this. When we finished, I took my gift upstairs and got back to work.

I hadn't been in the pub for long when Jeannie pushed through the door of the kitchen. "Got a minute?" she asked.

"Always for one of my favorite cooks." I put down the spray bottle of disinfectant cleaner I'd been using.

"We need you in the kitchen for a minute," she said.

Uh-oh. I hoped there wasn't a problem. "Is something wrong?"

Jeannie smiled and my fears were eased. "Nothing at all. We have something for you to try, and I couldn't wait any longer. I think I was annoying Jake because I kept asking when you'd be stopping in. He finally suggested I come and get you."

I smiled back. "It must be something good then, if you're that anxious for me to try it." I quickly rinsed the cleaner off my hands and followed her. In the kitchen, the aroma of onions, bacon, and German sausages was unmistakable. For a brief moment I was transported back to Germany. "Oh, wow," I said.

Jake grinned. "It's a little preview of the Oktoberfest offerings. I was trying to hold off until lunch, but Jeannie couldn't wait."

I glanced at the clock on the wall. It was just before eleven. "I'd say it's close enough to noon."

Kevin had three kinds of sausage on the grill. He cut samples for all of us and put them on plates. There was a pan on the range and Jeannie spooned out some German potato salad and placed it on the plates.

I must have been hungrier than I thought because I cleared my plate in record time. "What did you do to the wurst?" I asked Jake. "It was delicious."

"Marinated it in your brown ale," he said.

"We tried it in the lager first," Kevin chimed in, "but the ale gave it more flavor."

"These are going to be a big hit. Maybe we should consider adding them to the menu full time." I put my plate in the sink. "I'd better go finish up before we get busy."

Jeannie put a hand on my arm. "We have one more thing."

Jake opened one of the refrigerators and lifted something out. It was a round plate with a tall stainless steel cover over it. I couldn't see what it was. He placed it on the counter.

"Dessert?" I said.

"An Oktoberfest dessert," Jake said. He lifted the cover. It was a beautiful Black Forest cake.

Jake said, "It's Kurt's recipe."

"Oh, my." I couldn't get any other words out. Tears filled my eyes. This was the dessert Kurt had been trying to perfect when he'd been murdered. I thought about arriving at the pub that night and finding a bowl of cherries and whipped cream on the counter. About how I'd been angry with him because he hadn't been here after he'd called me to come down because he knew who had been vandalizing the brew house. He would have loved seeing his finished product. I found my voice. "It's gorgeous."

Jake put his arm around me. "I hope you're okay with it.

I thought since you were brewing Kurt's Oktoberfest beer, it was appropriate."

I smiled up at him through my tears. "It's wonderful. I wish I'd thought of it. Thank you."

Jake leaned down and kissed me.

Kevin cleared his throat. "Do you want to take that somewhere else? Between that and the cake, it's a little sickeningly sweet in here."

We all laughed at that.

Jake squeezed my shoulder. "I guess we'd better get back to work. Can't let the boss see us slacking off."

"I think I'll let it slide this time," I said. I left the kitchen with a smile on my face.

I was beginning to get nervous when I hadn't heard from Candy by two o'clock that afternoon. I called her cell phone but hung up when her voice mail picked up. I considered calling my dad to see what was going on, but he wasn't likely to know much since it wasn't his case. I hoped she had told Mitch everything. And that he believed her. If I hadn't known her so well, I'm not sure I would have believed that story coming from a woman who looked more like someone's grandma than a former secret agent.

I was putting some glasses away behind the bar a half hour later thinking about calling her again, when she and Tommy came through the door. I waved to them and pointed to two empty stools at the end of the bar. They crossed the pub and Tommy held the back of one of the seats for Candy, then took the other seat. They both looked tired—especially Candy.

Tommy was still dapper despite the circles under his eyes. He wore the same suit as last night minus the bowler hat and umbrella. Candy was dressed in her usual black and gold, but she'd toned it down for her interview with the police—plain black pants, pale yellow blouse, and a black blazer.

I was dying to hear what happened, but I played the good hostess first and asked them what they wanted to drink. I asked them if they were hungry and they both told me no.

After I drew a stout for Tommy and an iced tea for Candy, I said, "I've been trying to call you."

"I'm sorry about that," Candy said. "I only noticed a little while ago my phone was out of juice."

"How did everything go?"

"It's hard to say," Candy said. "I answered a million questions—more than once, I might add—and I got a strong reprimand."

"So you're in the clear?" A feeling of relief washed over me.

Candy and Tommy exchanged glances.

"Not quite," Tommy said.

I didn't like the sound of that. The relief I'd felt seconds before disappeared. "What do you mean?"

"Detective Raines said I was free to go," Candy said. "He didn't come right out and say so, but I got the impression I shouldn't leave town."

"You can't be serious," I said. "What did he say when you told him about Felix?"

They looked at each other again and Tommy spoke up. "Candace and I decided that it was better to keep Josef's identity to ourselves for the moment."

"That's ridiculous. Why would you do that?" I said to

Candy. "Felix or Josef or whatever his name is, is probably the person who killed Doodle. The police need to know this wasn't a random act and they certainly need to know you had nothing to do with it. Doodle was targeted because he knew too much. You should have told Mitch everything."

Candy rolled her eyes. "Don't have a conniption, Max. You're right that Josef might have killed Doodle, but if I told Detective Raines everything I told you—and by some miracle he actually believed me—he'd bring Josef in."

"Of course he would," I said. "That's what he's supposed to do."

"We don't want that to happen," Tommy said. "Not until we know why Josef is here and why he killed that man. If he is taken into custody, we'll never learn the truth."

I didn't believe that. "You don't know that. If he killed someone, he belongs in jail. And what about your safety, Candy? Don't forget that Felix recognized you. He could be coming after you as we speak."

Tommy downed the last of his stout. "We've taken precautions." He patted my hand. "I won't let anything happen to Candace. You have my word."

He sounded sincere, but I didn't know how he could possibly be sure of that. "You'd better be right." I shook my index finger at him. "If you let anything happen to Candy, you're going to have to answer to me."

Tommy grinned, and Candy laughed and said, "I wouldn't wish that on my worst enemy."

I didn't think it was funny. "I'm serious."

Candy leaned over the bar and gave me a one-armed hug. "I know you are and I appreciate it. There's nothing for you to worry about. I will be perfectly safe. You're still having that meeting tonight, aren't you?"

I nodded.

"Good. We'll tell you all about our plan then."

I watched them leave. Despite their reassurances, I was still worried. If Felix killed a man just for knowing too much, nothing was going to stop him from going after the woman who had shot him. Tommy may have been good at his job, but that was years ago and he was only one person. He was going to need help. He didn't know it yet, but Candy's friends were going to give it to him.

CHAPTER NINE

"Let's get this show on the road," Elmer said.

It was ten minutes after eight and Kristie, Daisy, Elmer, and I were sitting at a table in Jump, Jive & Java waiting for Candy and Tommy. Jake had gone to play pickup hockey, but I had promised to fill him in later.

"You know what Candy would tell you, Elmer," Kristie said.

"Yeah, she'd tell me we waited long enough."

Kristie shook her head. "Nope. She'd say, 'Keep your shirt on.'"

I grinned. "And Tommy would say, 'Don't get your knickers in a twist.'" I knew it didn't mean *be patient*, but it's all I could come up with that quickly. At least my British accent wasn't all that bad.

Daisy got into the act, too. "I have one. Hold your horses."

We continued in that vein with each suggestion becoming more and more ridiculous, and when Candy and Tommy entered a few minutes later, we were laughing so hard I had tears running down my cheeks.

"What's so funny?" Candy looked at Tommy, then back at us. "On second thought, I don't want to know." They each pulled out a chair and sat down. "Let's get this show on the road," she said, which was the same thing Elmer had said that started this whole thing. It was several minutes before we could control ourselves.

I wiped my eyes with a napkin. "Sorry about that. And you're right—you don't want to know."

Candy introduced her ex-husband to everyone, and before we knew it, Tommy and Elmer began exchanging stories. Candy nudged Tommy with her elbow. "You and Elmer can compare notes later. We have more important things to discuss right now."

"Bossy woman," Elmer said. "I see now why you two ain't married anymore."

I interrupted before things got any more out of hand. We'd wasted enough time already. Even though I'd given the others the basics, I asked Candy and Tommy to bring them up to date. Each time Elmer interrupted, he got *the look* from Candy and promptly shut up. They didn't go into quite as much detail as they had last night with Jake and me, but they made their point—Felix/Josef was dangerous. When they'd finished, I asked how we could help.

Candy tapped her fingernails on the table. "I don't want you to do anything other than keep your eyes open. Call me if you see Josef. It's only a matter of time before he realizes he really does know me, if he hasn't figured it out already."

I knew that's what she'd say. There was no way I was going to let her and Tommy deal with this situation themselves. It was much too dangerous. I was still a little put out that she'd held back the information about her past and what happened with Felix when she met with Mitch Raines. If she had told him everything, we wouldn't be in this position at all. The police would be handling it.

"No dice," Elmer said. "You're always butting into everyone else's business, it's about time we butt into yours."

"Elmer!" Daisy said.

He'd never in a million years admit that he was fond of Candy, and this was his way of saying he wanted to help. "What he means," I said, "is that you're always the first to help any of us out, so we're not going to let you do this alone." Elmer didn't correct me, so I knew I was right. "And there's no point in arguing with me, or any one of us. It won't do you any good. We're helping, and that's that."

Candy leaned back and crossed her arms. "Well. I guess you told me."

Tommy had been mostly silent until now. He leaned forward and rested his elbows on the table. "I know you all mean well, but I can't allow it. As a matter of fact, I won't allow it."

"And who put you in charge?" Elmer said. "I don't take orders from anyone. I'll do what I want."

"And that's your right, mate. But Candace and I will not involve amateurs in this endeavor."

Elmer leaned across the table toward Tommy. "Just who are you calling an amateur? I was jumping into enemy flak when you were in diapers. If it weren't for the good old U.S. of A., you limeys would be speaking German right now."

Candy slapped her hand on the table. "Oh, for goodness' sake. Stop acting like five-year-olds. Both of you."

Elmer sat back in his seat again.

"Sorry, love," Tommy said. "But I stand by my reluctance to involve anyone else in this."

"You need our help," I said. "You can't deal with this alone."

Candy put her hand on Tommy's arm. "Maybe we should rethink this. You don't know my friends like I do. Max has found not one, but two murderers before the police did."

"She's right," Kristie chimed in. "If you don't accept our help, we'll just go renegade on you."

"Yeah. I kind of like that idea," Daisy said with a grin. "Max's Marauders go rogue."

Tommy was quiet for a moment before he spoke up. "I must say, Candace, your friends are quite loyal. I see now why you speak so highly of them."

"Does that mean you'll accept our help?" I asked.

"With certain caveats," Candy said.

I wasn't sure what that meant exactly. "Do you have a plan?"

Kristie slipped out of her chair. "Before we start talking strategy, let me get everyone something to drink." She took our orders and Daisy got up to help her while Candy and I listened to Tommy and Elmer try to one-up each other with their tales of danger. There was a lot of eye-rolling back and forth between Candy and me. Fortunately, Kristie and Daisy returned with refreshments before either one of us ended up with headaches.

Candy sipped her iced tea then leaned back in her seat. "While the menfolk were yapping, I did some thinking."

I expected some kind of retort from Elmer or Tommy at this, but both were silent.

"Tommy and I had a plan but I want to change it slightly," she continued. "First, we know that Felix or Josef is a member of the band Max has hired to perform at her pub in a little over a week. And we know that they're now without a tuba or sousaphone player." She looked at me. "Will they cancel because of that?"

I shook my head. "No. I don't think so anyway. I called Bruce Hoffman to offer my condolences and he told me they were still planning on playing."

"Good," Candy said. "Since you already have an 'in' with them, maybe you could talk to him again. That will work better than me giving him a call. Find out where—or if— they're performing somewhere this coming weekend."

"I can certainly do that."

Candy continued. "If they are, Tommy and I will show up at the venue."

"Like hell you will," Elmer said. "You two do that, and you give away the whole deal. He'll recognize you for sure."

"I suppose you have a better plan, old man," Candy said.

"Darn tootin' I do." He pushed his cup aside and leaned on the table. "The band members know all of yinz, and that Felix fellow definitely knows you two. On the other hand, they've never seen me before."

He did have a point.

"Max can find out where they're going to be. I can go and talk to them on the pretense of wanting to hire them. I'll get talking to Felix and buy him a drink or two. Your old pal won't suspect an old geezer like me is trying to get information from him."

It was a great idea. I wished I'd thought of it.

Tommy shook his head. "I don't like it. It's one thing you all wanting to help, but you can't do this on your own. I won't put civilians in danger."

Candy put her hand on his arm again. "Tommy dear, we're all civilians now."

He sniffed. "I'm still a consultant. And I still have a security clearance. I haven't been completely put out to pasture."

"Like I have, you mean," Candy said.

"That's not what I meant, love. I mean that I'm still in touch with operatives all over the world. I can get help at a moment's notice."

Candy removed her hand from his arm. "You're not the only one with contacts, you know."

"Can you two have your lovers' spat later?" Elmer said. "We have work to do."

I took up the conversation. "I think Elmer's idea is a good one. He's right that if we all go in as a group, Candy is bound to get Felix's attention again. And no offense, Tommy, but if he sees the two of you together, he'll definitely make the connection."

Candy nodded. "She's right."

"Perhaps," Tommy said. "But I still don't care for it."

"It's really the best option at the moment," I said.

Tommy was silent again. Just when I thought he was going to refuse our help for the last time, he sighed. "It appears I'm outnumbered."

Candy patted his hand. "You'll get used to it."

We spent the next hour discussing strategy and made our plans for the weekend. First thing tomorrow morning I'd call Bruce Hoffman and set things in motion. If all went as planned, we'd know why Felix was in town and maybe even know who killed poor Doodle.

Jake's pickup hockey game ended early and he called to see if I wanted to get a late-night snack somewhere. Since his game had been north of the city, I agreed to meet him at the Eat'n Park in Etna, which was just across the 62nd Street Bridge over the Allegheny River. I had a sudden craving for a Smiley Cookie. The large sugar cookie with the frosted smiley face was one of the local chain's trademarked treats.

Jake's truck was already in the lot, and I parked beside it. I found him seated in a booth near the salad bar studying the menu. He looked up and smiled when I reached him. As always, his dimple made my stomach do a little flip. I kissed him on the cheek then slid into the seat across from him. "How was the game?"

"Good," he said. "A few of the regulars couldn't make it so we had to play three on three. When one of the guys had to leave, we called it a night."

I grinned. "Couldn't take it, huh?"

He returned my smile. "That about sums it up. I haven't had that much continuous ice time for a while. I'm probably going to feel it tomorrow."

"I doubt that. You skate all the time."

"True, but it's a little different in a game. I don't feel too bad right now, other than I'm starving."

He ended up ordering a Superburger Combo. I changed my mind about the Smiley Cookie when I looked at the menu. Instead, I got Grilled Stickies à la mode, which was basically grilled cinnamon bread topped with vanilla ice cream and a honey sauce.

After we'd ordered, Jake asked me how the meeting had gone.

"It went pretty well for the most part," I said. "Once we got Tommy and Elmer to quit trying to one-up each other, that is."

Jake laughed. "I can imagine how that went."

"At first, Tommy and Candy didn't want to involve us in their plans. They wanted to find out where the Deutschmen were playing this weekend and show up there—just the two of them."

"Felix would recognize them for sure."

I nodded. "That's exactly what we told them."

"So what's the plan now?"

"Elmer actually came up with it. He's the only one the band members have never seen. I'm going to call Bruce and find out their schedule. Elmer plans on going and talking to Felix to see if he can find out what he's up to."

"I'm not sure I like that plan. What about the rest of us? We can't just sit around and wait."

"We're not going to be waiting around," I said. "The rest of us can go and keep a low profile. Candy didn't like it, but we insisted that she and Tommy keep out of sight. I don't know if she'll listen, though. You know Candy."

The waitress brought our order then and there was no more discussion until Jake had finished practically inhaling his meal. I had only eaten half of my dessert by the time he finished, so I passed the remainder across the table to him.

"Are you sure you don't want this?" he asked.

I told him I'd had enough.

We didn't continue the discussion until Jake had paid the check and we were in the parking lot.

"I've been thinking," Jake said.

"Uh-oh. I thought I warned you about that," I teased.

"Very funny, O'Hara." He put his hands on my shoulders. "Maybe it's not such a bad idea if Candy and Tommy go and Felix sees them."

"But if he's as dangerous as they say—"

"Hear me out. The goal is to find out why Felix is here and if he killed Doodle, right?"

"Yes."

"Wouldn't it be better to just show our hand?" He didn't wait for an answer. "If he sees Candy and Tommy together, he'll know he was right that he'd recognized her. He's not going to make any kind of move in a public place. Even if he tries something, we'll all be watching and can stop him."

That was almost the same logic Candy had used earlier. It had been worth considering, but I didn't like putting Candy in any more danger than she was already in. Jake and I talked about it for a few more minutes, and in the end decided to stick with the original plan the rest of us had worked out earlier. We could break from the plan if Candy got bullheaded and did things her own way.

Before we said good-bye, Jake pulled me close and gave me a kiss that made my toes curl. Between worrying about Candy and thinking about that kiss, I was definitely going to have trouble sleeping tonight.

T he next morning, after I'd checked the fermenters and prepared to brew another batch of IPA, I went to my office and called Bruce Hoffman's number. When his voice mail picked up, I had a sudden revelation and went back out to the pub to retrieve the newspaper I'd placed on the bar when I came in. I pulled out the second section and turned to the obituaries, wishing I'd thought of it sooner. Doodle's funeral was in an hour, but I was in luck. His graveside service was right here in Lawrenceville at the Allegheny Cemetery. If I rushed home and quickly changed clothes, I might just make it. I scribbled a note for Jake, who was due in shortly, and headed out.

I had ten minutes to spare when I made it to the Butler Street entrance to the cemetery. The entranceway wasn't the ordinary gate you'd see at most cemeteries. It was a massive stone gatehouse complete with turrets, and it was larger than some houses. It was appropriate considering Allegheny Cemetery was the final resting place for many local dignitaries such as members of the Mellon and Carnegie families. Composer Stephen Foster and actress Lillian Russell were buried there, as well as several congressmen and the owner of the old Eberhardt and Ober Brewery. There were soldiers buried there from every war dating back to the French and Indian War. One of the most notorious residents was Harry Thaw, who murdered the husband of Evelyn Nesbit, the original Gibson Girl.

Once I passed under the archway, I realized that I had no idea which way to go. The cemetery sat on three hundred acres and had fifteen miles of road. Finding Doodle's service would be akin to finding a needle in a haystack. It could be an hour or more before I found the right spot if I drove around. The service would be long over by then.

I pulled in front of the administration office and went in. It only took seconds for a woman to point out the location on a map. I was back in my car and on my way in short order. Doodle's gravesite was at the end of one of the winding side roads. Besides the hearse, there were only four vehicles lined up, and I parked behind the last one—a white cargo van—and got out of my car.

The service had just begun when I silently joined the others. Bruce Hoffman, Manny Levin, and Felix Holt were all there. I had half expected Felix to be a no-show—especially if he had been the one who killed Doodle. Bruce glanced up and gave me a nod to acknowledge my presence. Besides the man speaking at the head of the grave, the only other mourners were two women. They looked like they were related to each other, but one appeared older by a few years. The older woman was dry-eyed, but the younger one kept dabbing at her eyes with a lace handkerchief.

The brief service was over five minutes later, and I moved around the grave to offer my condolences to the band members. I shook hands with all three while trying to pay close attention to Felix without being obvious about it. "Thanks for coming," Bruce said.

"Yes, thank you," Manny said.

"It's been a terrible loss," Felix added.

He sounded as if he meant it, but if he'd been as good a spy as Candy and Tommy said, I wouldn't expect anything less. He'd have to be an excellent actor.

Bruce motioned toward the women. "Have you met Doodle's sisters?"

For some reason, I had been under the impression that he didn't have any family. "No, I haven't."

"This is Rhonda," Bruce said, pointing to the older woman. She appeared to be in her fifties, with sandy hair touched with white. She was tall, slender, and immaculately dressed in a navy sheath and spectator pumps.

"And this is Paisley." She couldn't have been more than thirty and I wondered about the difference in ages. Then again, Doodle had been in his forties—right in the middle of the sisters. Paisley had dark blond hair that had been highlighted with at least three different colors. It was straight and hung halfway down her back. She wore a black maxi skirt with a white sleeveless shell and white sandals.

I shook their hands. "You have my sympathy. I didn't know your brother well, but he seemed like a good man."

Rhonda stared me down, apparently sizing me up. "How exactly did you know Walter? You don't look like any of his previous bimbos."

Paisley gasped. "How could you say such a thing! Walter's girlfriends were all nice people."

Rhonda rolled her eyes. "For heaven's sake, Paisley. Get a grip. Our dear departed brother chose women like he was choosing a paint color. The flashier the color, the more he liked it." She turned to me. "It was nice meeting you, but I have to run."

Speechless, I watched her walk away.

"Please excuse my sister," Paisley said. "She's just upset."

Manny Levin snorted. "Yeah, upset that old Doodle didn't leave her a dime."

"That's not nice," Paisley said. "Walter loved both of us."

Bruce patted her on the arm. "We know he did. He talked about you all the time."

"He did?" She sounded surprised.

"Yes," Felix said. "He did."

"He promised to take care of me. And he would have, too. But now we'll never know what might have been." Paisley burst into tears.

While Bruce comforted her, Manny and Felix began walking toward their cars. I was torn between staying behind to talk more with Paisley or following them. Felix was the real reason I was here, so I followed. Manny was already in his car when I reached the road, but Felix was taking his time unlocking his car door.

"I'm glad I caught up with you," I said. "I was going to talk to Bruce, but he's busy with Doodle's sister at the moment."

Felix turned to face me. "What did you want to talk to him about?"

"My Oktoberfest celebration next weekend. If you're going to cancel, I need to know so I can find other musicians."

"We will be there. We can manage without the sousa-phone. A ridiculous instrument in my opinion."

I kind of agreed with him on that. "That's a relief. It would be hard to find a replacement—especially one as good as the Deutschmen." I figured it wouldn't hurt to throw in a compliment.

"Thank you, but I'm sure you'd manage."

I didn't know what to say next. I couldn't very well come out and say, *Are you here to kill my friend, and oh, by the way, did you kill Doodle?* Then I remembered what I wanted to find out. "Are you performing anywhere this weekend? I'd like to bring my boyfriend to hear you."

"We perform every weekend. We're very much in de-mand, especially at this time of year. There's a fall festival at Hartwood Acres on Saturday and we are the entertain-ment for the evening. You should come." He paused. "And bring all your friends. All of them. I would like to see them again."

A chill went through me as I watched him get in his car and drive away. He hadn't said anything threatening, but his tone had definitely changed when he said he wanted me to bring my friends. Maybe I was reading too much into it, but it was clear to me that by *friends*, he really meant Candy.

Which meant that he knew exactly who she was.

CHAPTER TEN

ops opened one eye when I stopped at home to change clothes again. She wasn't used to being disturbed twice in the same morning. She yawned and burrowed deeper into the comforter on my bed. I patted her on the head, then slipped back into the old jeans and T-shirt I'd worn earlier since I was planning on brewing today.

The day was warm and sunny so I decided to leave my car at home and walk to the brewery. Besides, it was the lunch hour, and I doubted I'd find a parking place that wasn't blocks away. I'd been tempted to use Pittsburgh's version of a reserved parking space—the parking chair—on a couple of occasions, but couldn't bring myself to chance leaving one of the pub chairs on the street or in the lot. I wasn't even sure if it was legal, even though people in congested areas did it all the time. It was especially common in the winter to prevent anyone else from parking in the spot the resident had just shoveled out. The funny thing was, Pittsburghers respected the parking chair. I'd never heard of anyone moving one to park.

When I reached my stretch of Butler Street, I noticed some activity across the street from the brew house where three boutiques had been up until four months ago. I was more than happy that two of the buildings had recently found new owners. The empty storefronts had been a daily reminder of Kurt's murder and all that had happened this past May. One of the new stores was in the process of becoming a tea shop, and the other was a newly opened yarn and fabric store called Simply Stitches. And now it looked as if the third place had a new owner. I crossed the street to see what the new shop might be.

The front door was propped open. Workmen were building shelves on the side walls, and before I could even say hello, my parents' neighbor, Marcus Crawford, walked out of the back room.

He grinned at me. "Hi, neighbor," he said.

I returned his greeting and shook his hand. "This is a surprise. Why didn't you mention this on Sunday at my parents' house? I would have given you a proper welcome to the neighborhood." All the talk on Sunday had been about his partner's art gallery and newest acquisition. He'd never said a word about opening a shop—especially one so close to the brew house.

"I didn't want to jinx anything. The closing was only on Tuesday, and up until then, I wasn't sure it was really going to happen. It was hard not to say anything, especially knowing your pub was across the street."

"What's your plan for this place?" I asked, wondering what kind of store a former college football player whose most recent job was in banking would be opening.

He reached behind what had been the sales counter in the former This and That. I pushed the thought of the last time I was in this building out of my mind. Marcus lifted a large rectangular sign and placed it on top of the counter. "Does this answer your question?"

I took a step closer to the counter. *Good & Healthy.* "So it's a health food store?"

Marcus smiled again. "It's much more than that. In addition to the usual health food, I'll have vitamins and other supplements, fitness products, maybe even some seminars on healthy living."

"That's wonderful," I said. "I think it will be a big hit. There's nothing like it in this neighborhood."

"Thanks. I appreciate the vote of confidence. It's a big change for me, but something I've always wanted to do."

"I know what it's like to follow that dream. It's not always easy, but it's very fulfilling."

Marcus nodded. "It helps that Philip is so supportive," he said. "I talked about doing something like this for years. I guess he got tired of the talk and finally convinced me to ditch the bank job and do this." He said he hoped to open up by the end of September or beginning of October. We talked for another minute or two, then I excused myself and headed back across the street.

As usual, Nicole had everything under control. Most of the tables were filled and the delicious aromas filling the air reminded me I hadn't eaten anything yet today. I headed to the kitchen.

Kevin Bruno looked up as I entered. "Uh-oh. Someone's hungry again."

"You bet I am."

"I hope you're not looking for that cake, because we ate it," he said.

"Who ate it?" Jeannie quipped.

"Okay. I confess," Kevin said. "It was all me. I ate it."

I laughed. "I won't fire you for that, but consider yourself warned," I teased. "As the good sisters used to say when I was in school, this is going on your permanent record."

Kevin looked aghast. "Really?"

I shook my head. "I'm teasing you, Kev. Although the nuns really did say that."

"Whew," he said. "You had me going there for a minute."

Jake was chopping green peppers and I gave him a quick kiss.

"How did it go this morning?" he asked.

"It was interesting." I picked up a pepper chunk and took a bite. "Doodle has two sisters."

"I guess you got to talk to them."

"Yes, I did." The pepper was tasty, but it wasn't enough. "Rhonda and Paisley." I opened the cupboard where I kept my stash of peanut butter.

Jeannie looked up from where she was assembling a burger platter. "Paisley? What kind of a name is that?"

I opened the jar of peanut butter and reached for a spoon. "It's different, that's for sure."

"Is that really going to be your lunch?" Jake pointed to the peanut butter.

"What's wrong with peanut butter on a spoon? It's very nutritious."

Kevin laughed and Jeannie rolled her eyes.

Jake wiped his hands on a towel. "It's not enough to eat. I'll make you a sandwich."

"But I like peanut butter."

He smiled. "I know you do. But brewers shall not live on peanut butter alone."

Kevin said, "How about a burger? I have a couple of extras here."

"If I have to." Actually, it sounded really good.

Jake quickly assembled a burger with all the fixings on one of his homemade pretzel buns. The lunch orders had slowed down by this time so Jake made one for himself and joined me in the office for lunch. He must have been as hungry as I was because we both wolfed down most of our lunch before we talked more about Doodle's funeral. "Who else was there?" he asked.

I filled him in on my little talk with Felix. "Nothing he said was threatening in the least. Maybe I'm reading too much into it because of what Candy said about him, but I got the impression he knows exactly who she is and he'd like nothing better than to run into her again. He practically insisted I bring my friends to see them play."

"Have you told Candy yet?"

"No, and I'm not sure what to tell her. I have a feeling even though we planned otherwise, she'll show up at Hartwood Acres anyway. I know it's a big estate, but there are plenty of places he'd be able to corner her—especially if he's able to get her into the mansion."

"The festival is outdoors, though, isn't it?"

I nodded. "But the house could still be open."

"We'll just have to make sure Tommy knows all this as well. Maybe he'll be able to keep her away from Felix."

"I don't envy him. When Candy sets her mind on something, there's no stopping her."

"What were Doodle's sisters like?" he asked.

I told him that Rhonda seemed to be a bit of a snob. "She wanted to know if I was one of Doodle's bimbos."

Jake laughed. "Seriously? Knowing you, that's pretty funny."

"You don't think I could be a bimbo?"

"Not on your life, O'Hara."

I tried giving him a sultry look but a pickle slice fell from the last piece of my sandwich and landed on my desk. "Looks like you're right." I picked up the pickle and wiped my hands with a napkin.

Jake gathered up our debris and tossed it in the trash then pulled me to my feet. "You'll never be a bimbo, but you've got that sexy look down pat."

The heat in the room jumped up a couple of notches. "Oh, really."

He pulled me closer. "Definitely. Now what should we do about that?"

I wrapped my arms around his waist. "I have a pretty good idea."

J spent most of the afternoon in the brewery. I had planned on brewing the India pale ale the same way I always did but decided at the last minute to change the recipe a bit. I switched around some of the hops I usually used and changed some of the amounts. Because I wasn't a big fan of the bitterness of most IPAs, I was always cautious not to overdo it with the hops. I'd been told more than once that my IPA wasn't "hoppy" enough. This time, I decided to throw caution to the wind. Hopefully I wouldn't have to dump the whole batch down the drain. I'd know in about two weeks.

Nicole went off duty at five since she had a class that evening, so I took over at the bar. It was slow enough that I had time to think in between drawing drafts and seating and chatting with customers. My thoughts went back to the funeral that morning and how different Doodle's sisters were from each other. What had Manny Levin said about Rhonda? She was angry that her brother hadn't left her anything. From the way she was dressed and the car she drove, it seemed to me that she was the one with money, not her brother. I had seen Doodle's house, and it certainly wasn't the home of anyone who was well off. Plus, how much could he possibly make performing with the Deutschmen? Maybe he had another source of income I didn't know about. If he had, it sure wasn't obvious.

Then there was Paisley. Where Rhonda seemed to be hard and unemotional, I got the opposite impression of Paisley. I could imagine Doodle and Paisley getting along just fine. Doodle and Rhonda—not so much. I tried to remember what Paisley had said about her brother. Something about Doodle promising to take care of her. I wondered what that meant. I didn't have any more time to ponder that because Marcus Crawford and Philip Rittenhouse entered the pub and were heading my way.

I gave them a big smile. "Welcome to the Allegheny Brew House."

"I came down to drag Marcus out of his shop," Philip said, "and we were both hungry, so . . ." He shrugged.

Marcus grinned. "Philip knew I'd be there all night if he left it up to me."

"Let me get you a table," I said. I grabbed a couple of menus and led them to a table near one of the front windows.

They asked about the beers and I gave them the rundown. Marcus chose an IPA and Philip a brown ale. When I returned with them, Philip asked if I had a minute.

"Sure," I said. "What can I do for you?"

"Nothing," Philip said. "I just wanted to let you know that I'll be unveiling the Vermeer at the gallery tomorrow evening since my client is coming to town and I'd like to invite you and Jake."

"That's wonderful," I said. "I'd love to, but I don't think I can make it. My manager is off again tomorrow night."

"That's disappointing," Philip said. "You seemed to be so interested in it."

Marcus asked, "Can you get someone to cover for you?"

"Maybe. I can talk to Mike. He covers for me sometimes. I'd really love to see that painting."

"If you miss the unveiling, you'll still have a chance to

see it. The owner has granted permission for me to display it for the next month."

"I take it that it's been authenticated," I said.

Philip nodded. "I'm waiting for a chemical analysis yet, but the three experts who have examined it believe that it is most likely a Vermeer. That's good enough for my buyer."

"And for you, too?"

"I'd rather wait until I have the results of the analysis, but my client doesn't. Besides, I have no reason to doubt the experts."

More customers entered the pub and headed for the bar. "I've got to get back to work. If I don't make it tomorrow night, I will definitely stop in as soon as I can," I said.

There was a steady crowd over the next few hours, and I didn't get a chance to talk to Philip or Marcus again. They stopped briefly on the way out to say that they loved the place and would be back soon. It began to slow down around nine, and shortly after that, Candy and Tommy stopped in.

I still didn't like the idea of telling Candy about the Deutschmen performing this weekend. Like I'd said to Jake, I knew her well enough that despite what she'd agreed to last night, she'd want to be in the thick of things. I'd just have to make sure she wasn't.

"Any news?" Candy asked as she slid onto one of the oak bar stools. "Are they performing this weekend?"

"Hello to you, too," I said.

Tommy smiled as he took the seat beside Candy. "So sorry, Maxine. Candace is a bit anxious."

"I am not. I'm perfectly fine."

"No, you're not, love."

Before it turned into a full-blown spat, I asked if I could get them something.

"I suppose you don't have anything harder than ale?" Tommy asked.

"I'm afraid not." I had no plans at the moment to add a full bar—after all, it was a brewpub. *Brew* being the operative word.

Tommy slipped a stainless steel flask from his pocket. "I believe I'll just have some tea then."

I laughed. "Are you always so prepared?"

"Of course I am, my dear."

Candy's fingernails had been doing a dance on the bar top and she stopped tapping. "I don't mean to be rude, but can we get back to the subject at hand?"

"In a minute," I said as I placed an iced tea in front of her, then got a mug of hot water and a tea bag for Tommy.

"If you don't talk soon, I'll have you banned from the bakery," Candy said.

"You wouldn't."

She gave me her famous look. "Just try me."

I didn't think she really meant it, but I wasn't going to chance it. "I went to Doodle's funeral this morning."

"And?" Candy said.

"I met Doodle's sisters."

"He had sisters?"

Now I knew why she didn't like it when I kept interrupting her. It was annoying. I was going to have to remember that. "Two of them." I told them about Rhonda and Paisley and my impressions of them. "The band members were also there—including Felix."

Candy jabbed Tommy with her elbow. "I told you we should have gone to the funeral."

"That wouldn't have accomplished anything, love," he said.

"Yes, it would have," she said. "He'd know we were on to him."

Tommy sipped his doctored tea. "Which is exactly what we don't want to do."

I broke in. "I had a chance to talk to Felix as everyone was leaving. I'd planned on talking to Bruce, but he was busy consoling Paisley so I caught up to Felix right before he got into his car."

"What did he say?" Candy asked.

I'd half expected her to berate me and tell me it was too dangerous for me to talk to him but she didn't. "They're playing on Saturday at Hartwood Acres' fall festival. He suggested I come and see them, and he mentioned I should bring my friends. He didn't come right out and say it, but I think he specifically meant you. I have the feeling he figured out how he knows you."

"I'm not surprised," Tommy said. "Josef was very astute. I knew it wouldn't take him long to realize that."

Candy tapped her nails on the bar top again. "This may require a change in plans. We had been counting on them being at a much smaller venue but since it's a festival—"

"No," I said. "You're not going."

She raised an eyebrow. "That's a switch—you telling me what to do."

"It's about time someone did."

"Candace is right." Tommy pushed his cup aside. "If this

is a large festival with a crowd of people, it may be in our best interest to attend."

I didn't like the idea. Not at all. "What if Felix sees you?"

"It doesn't really matter," Candy said. "He already knows who I am. He probably knows exactly where to find me. He hasn't tried anything yet."

"That doesn't mean he won't," I said.

"Max, I know you're worried about me," she said, "but there's no need to be. I still know how to take care of myself."

"I won't let anything happen to her," Tommy added. "A large venue is just the ticket. And he won't expect to see me." He grinned. "I can't wait to see the look on his face."

It was a bad idea. Very, very bad. Felix had once tried to kill Candy and Tommy, and there was no guarantee he wouldn't try it again. I reminded them of this, and that he was most likely the person who killed Doodle. But as hard as I tried, I wasn't able to talk them out of attending the festival.

I had a feeling something terrible was going to happen and there was absolutely nothing I could do about it.

CHAPTER ELEVEN

Jake and I were the last to leave the brew house that night. Since I had walked to work, he offered to drive me home, and I accepted. We hadn't had much time to talk since we'd had lunch together so I filled him in on Candy's and Tommy's latest idea. "I really don't think she should go," I said when I'd finished.

"I'm not so sure," Jake said. "Do you really think Felix would try anything in a public place with hundreds of people around?"

"Maybe not, but look what happened at the brews and burgers festival this summer. That was a public place and it didn't deter that killer. Why take the chance?"

He reached over and squeezed my hand. "We can make

sure she's safe. If one of us has eyes on her the whole time, it will be fine."

We'd reached my parking lot by then and I asked him if he wanted to come in.

"Not tonight," he said. "I forgot to tell you earlier, but remember the high school practice I told you about the other day?"

I said I did.

"I got a call from the coach and he asked if I'd be interested in helping them out temporarily with practices. The assistant coach just had emergency surgery to have his appendix removed and they're kind of stuck."

"That sounds like fun—and something you'd enjoy. I hope you told him yes."

"I'm glad you think that, because I told him I'd be happy to help. It won't interfere with work at all since it's just for practices. I wouldn't have to go to the games unless I wasn't working then. The only bad thing is that the practices are at four in the morning."

"Ugh. That's early."

"Yeah. But that's why I'm not coming up tonight. First practice is tomorrow." Jake grinned. "I've got to get my beauty sleep."

Funny guy. "If you're still awake by tomorrow night, I have a proposition for you."

"Does it involve some lacy getup?"

"That depends on what you mean by *lacy getup*," I said, although I knew perfectly well what was on his mind.

He put his arm around me and leaned closer. "Black lace,

stockings, minimal coverage . . ." He pulled me closer. "Is that what you had in mind?"

"Well . . . not exactly." I gave him an innocent grin. "Although the black and the stockings might work. But that minimal coverage thing is right out."

"You're killing me, O'Hara."

I told him about the unveiling of the painting at Philip's gallery. "If I can get Mike to cover the bar, I'd like to go."

"I don't need to be in the kitchen, so count me in. If I get bored, Marcus and I can talk sports."

We chatted for another minute or two, then Jake kissed me good night and I headed inside.

𝕴 was in luck. As soon as I'd said good-bye to Jake, I'd texted Mike and he said he'd be available to cover for me. I was free to go to the unveiling of the Vermeer at Philip's gallery. I'd never gone to an event like this before and had no idea of how to dress. The only time I'd seen anything like it was on TV. So instead of relying on some TV writer's idea of what one should wear to a gallery, I did something better the first thing in the morning—I called my mother.

She was surprised to hear from me so early. "Is everything all right, sweetie?"

"Everything's fine," I said. "I just wanted to ask your advice. Philip invited Jake and me to the gallery tonight and I don't know what to wear. How do people dress for these things?"

"I don't think Philip will care what you wear," she said. "That said, it's likely to be very formal."

"That's what I was afraid of." I had some seldom-worn dresses in my closet, but none of them even came close to being formal.

"How busy are you today?" she asked.

"Not very. I'm not brewing today, and the pub is well staffed. I planned to lock myself in my office and do paperwork."

"I know something that will be a lot more fun than doing paperwork." I could hear the smile in her voice. "I'd say a mother-daughter shopping trip is in order. I need something to wear, too."

By noon, we both had new dresses. And shoes. Mom found a sophisticated-looking black sheath with lace sleeves that reached to her elbow. I'd had a harder time picking something. Everything I tried on made me look like I was attending my high school prom. Our last stop was a boutique that sold vintage and vintage replica clothing. As soon as I saw the silver-beaded, 1920s-style dress, I knew that was the one. I tried it on and it fit like a dream. I felt like a flapper from the twenties. I almost had a heart attack when I saw the price, though. It was three times what I wanted to spend. I rationalized it by telling myself I hadn't bought anything besides jeans, T-shirts, or sweaters for years. I deserved it. I picked up the matching T-strap shoes and handed over my credit card before common sense got the best of me.

We were both starving by that time, so we headed to a nearby Italian restaurant for lunch. Once we'd ordered, Mom said, "That was fun. We should do this more often."

"I'm okay with going to lunch more often, but I can't

afford any more shopping," I said. "I can't believe I spent that much on a dress."

"Do you like it, though?"

I gave her a big smile. "I love it."

"That's the important thing. You wouldn't want to buy something you didn't love just because it was cheaper. But you're right—you don't want to do it too often." There was a twinkle in her eye. "I'll bet Jake is going to like it."

I felt my face turn fiery red. Not that it mattered to Mom—she knew how I felt about him. As a matter of fact, she'd known how I felt since I was about twelve years old. And she'd never once called it puppy love, or told me to get over it. She had always respected my feelings. Even when my crush made a reappearance when I hired Jake to be my chef, she supported me. She'd even encouraged me to tell him how I felt. Of course I ignored her, convinced that Jake couldn't possibly feel the same way. I was wrong about that, thank goodness.

Just then, the waitress brought glasses of water with lemon to the table. We thanked her, and once she was gone, I said, "I'm not sure what he'll think. We usually end up at casual places, so he's never seen me dressed up before."

She reached across the table and patted my hand. "You're going to knock his socks off. He'll love it."

"I hope so. He's wearing a suit. He doesn't have to do that much anymore." I hadn't even had to suggest it to him, which was good. I would never tell him how to dress—he'd had enough of that from his ex-fiancée. She'd have had a hissy fit that he was wearing a suit from off the rack at Kohl's and not a designer tuxedo.

While we ate, I filled my mom in on some things that

had happened since I'd last seen her on Sunday. She already knew from my dad that I had found Doodle's body on Monday, but the rest of the story was a big surprise.

"I can't believe Candy kept all that to herself for so many years," Mom said. "And to think she also had a husband no one knew about. Did she tell you why they broke up?"

I shook my head. "And I haven't had the chance to ask her. It's so apparent that they still care for each other. I don't get why they're not together."

"She'll tell you eventually."

"I hope so." I pushed my empty plate aside. "It would be nice if Tommy stuck around. I think he's good for Candy." I smiled. "He doesn't let her boss him around."

Mom laughed. "I'd love to meet him. Do you think the two of them would come to Sunday dinner if I asked?"

I said that I thought they might, then told her some of our plans for our Saturday jaunt to Hartwood Acres. I left out anything that might sound too dangerous. I didn't want her to worry, but she probably would anyway.

All in all, it was an enjoyable outing. We parted company at the pub, where I gathered up my purchases and took them inside. As I sat down at my desk to finish some paperwork, I realized I was smiling to myself. Mom was right—we definitely needed to do this more often.

Mike came in at five thirty. He'd helped out numerous times already and he loved tending bar. I could have called Nicole to work instead, but she did enough extra duty and I wanted her to enjoy her night off.

I didn't have to be at the gallery until eight. Jake was picking me up at my apartment at seven thirty, so I had plenty of time to get ready. He'd been trying to find out what was in the large bag hanging in my office all afternoon. He kept guessing wrong, with most of his guesses leaning toward the risqué. The few times I left my office to check on things in the brewery, I locked my door so he wouldn't be tempted to take a peek and ruin my surprise.

While I was getting ready, Hops decided that the shoe box was hers. I had taken the shoes from the box, removed the balled-up tissue paper that was inside, and tossed the paper balls back into the box. When I came back to the bedroom after my shower, the paper was scattered all over the floor and Hops was lounging in the box. I shook my head and laughed, once again glad I hadn't spent money on a cat bed.

I put on a little more makeup than I normally did, adding some gray eye shadow and plum lipstick. I usually went bare-faced or slapped on some blush and mascara. I wasn't sure what to do with my hair since it was so short. I used a little gel and fluffed it with my fingers. It would have to do. When I finally slipped the dress on, I checked my appearance in the full-length mirror on the back of my bedroom door. I couldn't remember the last time I'd gotten so dressed up. I hardly recognized myself.

"What do you think, Hops?"

She glanced up from her new shoe box and yawned. She wasn't impressed.

The doorbell rang as I finished putting on my shoes. The heels were only two inches high, but they felt strange because I always wore flats or sneakers. I was glad the heels weren't so high that I'd have trouble walking or even trip over my own feet.

When I opened the door, Jake was definitely more impressed than Hops had been. "Wow," he said.

I did a little pirouette. At least I think that's what they'd called it when Mom signed me up for ballet lessons when I was five. I'd preferred to spin around and around until I got dizzy and fell over. The ballet teacher frowned on that. I'd only made it through three classes. "What do you think?"

"No one is going to be looking at that painting tonight. They'll all be staring at you."

"You look great," I said. "Very handsome." He was dressed in a charcoal suit with a white shirt and red tie.

"I'm happy I didn't throw out all my old suits." He took both of my hands in his. "If anyone tries to hit on you tonight, I'm going to body-check them."

I laughed. "I'd like to see that. Just not into the painting, please."

The Gallery on Ellsworth was only a block from the parking garage—easy walking distance even in my dress shoes. Jake offered to drop me off, but I wouldn't hear of it. There was already quite a crowd inside the gallery when we arrived. Philip Rittenhouse stood inside the glass door greeting everyone as they arrived. He shook Jake's hand and kissed me on the cheek and told me I looked ravishing. Maybe I should dress up more often.

Many of the attendees were public figures. I recognized

a few of them, including Ginger Alvarado and her city councilman husband, Edward. Ginger had been the organizer of the Three Rivers Brews and Burgers Festival that we'd participated in over the summer. I pointed them out to Jake and we headed that way.

Ginger greeted us as if she were the First Lady. "I'm so happy to see you both," she said. "You remember Edward, don't you?"

"Of course," I said. "How are you both?"

"Very well," Edward said. "Fabulous event, don't you think?"

I didn't get a chance to respond because a reporter came up to speak to him.

Ginger smiled. "That reporter is about to get a scoop. Edward has decided to definitely run for County Executive."

Jake and I offered our congratulations.

"I hope this means we'll have your support." She looked at us expectantly.

"Sure thing," Jake said.

Ginger clapped her hands together. "Wonderful! We'll have all kinds of volunteer opportunities—fund-raising, going door to door . . ."

He put his hand under my elbow and squeezed. I took it to mean, *Get me out of this conversation and quick.*

Fortunately I spotted my mother across the room just then. "Oh, there's Mom over there. We'd better go over. It was nice seeing you again, Ginger." I turned and hurried away with Jake right behind me before she even opened her mouth to say good-bye.

"That was close," Jake said. "If I would have known she

wanted free labor and not just a vote, I would have kept my mouth shut."

"Look. Dad and the mayor just joined Mom."

A waiter carrying a tray of champagne was nearby, and Jake took two glasses from him. He passed one to me. "If we're talking politics, we're going to need these."

"Don't worry. The mayor is just a regular guy. You'll like him." We reached my parents and the mayor.

"Well, look at my little girl," Dad said with a smile after he gave me a kiss. "Beautiful. You look just like your mother."

"Many years ago, maybe," Mom said.

She introduced Jake to the mayor and they immediately started talking hockey. I was glad because it gave me a chance to talk to my dad. I asked him about the investigation into Doodle's murder.

"As far as I know, Mitch hasn't turned up anything new."

"Did he say anything about his interview with Candy? Is she still a suspect? Has he talked to the other band members?"

Dad sighed. "It's not my case, sweetie. Maybe you should ask Mitch."

I was disappointed. Even though Dad wasn't the investigator, I had hoped he'd at least heard something. I'd give Detective Raines a call tomorrow. He wasn't under any obligation to tell me anything, but maybe he would anyway. I finished my champagne and set the glass down on a small table.

Philip clinked his glass with a small fork he'd taken from the hors d'oeuvre table. "May I have everyone's attention, please?"

We all turned his way.

He stood beside an easel covered with a white cloth. "Thank you all for coming. This gallery has been a dream of mine for many years. Too many, if you ask Marcus."

His partner was behind him and off to the side, and he grinned. "Way too many." Soft laughter buzzed through the room.

"I'm doubly blessed," Philip continued, "that tonight not only marks the opening of the gallery, but also the unveiling of what is one of Johannes Vermeer's so-called 'lost paintings.' I won't bore you with details, but according to the research of various art scholars over the last few centuries, there are at least six documented works of art by Vermeer that haven't been seen since the late seventeenth century. They were mentioned in an auction catalog from a patron's estate in the year 1696. The painting that I've acquired for a buyer is believed to be the one identified in the catalog as *Face by Vermeer* and is thought to have been painted before 1660." He smiled. "In other words, this painting predates the famous *Girl with a Pearl Earring* by at least four or five years."

I whispered to my mother, "This is so fascinating. Has Philip learned any more about where it came from or how it was found?"

"Only that it was found in Austria hidden in the wall of a house that had been torn down," Mom said. "A private collector had passed it down through the family over many years and hid it in the wall from the Germans during the Second World War."

Philip moved behind the painting and placed his hands

on the white cloth that covered it. "Without further ado, I present *Face by Vermeer.*" He lifted the cover to reveal the painting to loud applause.

A frisson of excitement went through me. The thought that this painting was over three hundred and fifty years old thrilled me. I had seen pictures of the *Girl with a Pearl Earring* many times and this one was similar, yet different. This girl faced in the opposite direction and there were other differences, but it was apparent that Vermeer had gotten the inspiration for the later painting from this one.

Jake stood beside me and reached for my hand. "She's almost as pretty as you," he said.

A flash of blond hair caught my eye as a woman moved behind him. I did a double take. It couldn't be.

"Hello, Jake," she said.

He spun around. "Victoria?" His surprise quickly turned to anger. "What the hell are you doing here?"

CHAPTER TWELVE

That was an excellent question. What was Jake's ex-fiancée doing here? Had she come to try and take him back? Or to just make his life miserable? From what he'd told me, those things could be one and the same.

Victoria's laugh was probably pleasant to most people, but it was like fingernails on a chalkboard to me. "Surprised to see me, darling?" she said.

Jake let go of my hand and put his arm around my waist. "Don't call me that. And yeah, I'm surprised. I thought the only time you left New York was to fly to Europe or the West Coast. Why are you here?"

Instead of answering his question, she gave me the once-over. And frankly, I did the same to Miss Supermodel. She was almost as tall as Jake's six foot three. Her blond hair hung past her shoulders, the waves falling in perfect symmetry on both sides. I resisted the urge to reach up and touch my own hair, which I was sure was sticking up in a thousand different places. She wore a baby blue, mid-calf-length dress that hugged her body, and I doubted that she wore anything under it.

"You must be the girl brewer that I've heard so much about." She reached out her hand, and after I checked to be sure she wasn't holding a snake or something, I reluctantly shook it.

"I'm Max," I said. Like she didn't know that already.

Victoria smiled at Jake. "She's cute, but you've really come down in the world." She looked back at me. "And I guess you think you've latched on to quite the catch. He's definitely a step up from beer-guzzling steel workers."

If I killed her now, I wondered if it would be justifiable homicide. I curled my fingers into fists.

I had the feeling she wanted Jake to make a scene but he wasn't falling for her bait. He pulled me closer. "How about answering my question?" he said.

She was holding a glass of champagne and she took a sip before answering. "Isn't it obvious?"

Jake said, "The only obvious thing is that you're a conniving little bit—"

"Do you two know each other?" Philip had joined us. I hadn't even seen him approach.

Victoria gave Philip a dazzling smile. "Intimately."

At the same time, Jake answered, "Unfortunately."

I liked Jake's answer better.

"I hadn't realized that," Philip said, "or I would have invited Max and Jake to dinner with us."

Victoria placed her hand on Philip's arm and gazed adoringly at him. She did know he was gay, didn't she? "I didn't know he'd be here. This isn't the usual company he keeps these days. Besides, I adore surprises."

"We'll have to all get together another time then," Philip said.

Jake mumbled, "When hell freezes over."

I was the only one who heard him and I suppressed a smile.

Victoria still had her hand on Philip's arm and he placed his other hand over hers. "It's time to introduce you."

She gave a catty smile to Jake. "I'll be delighted and honored to let everyone know that I'm the owner of that painting."

Jake and I were both too shocked to say a word. We watched them head toward the painting. A waiter passed by and Jake grabbed a glass, downed it in one gulp, and put the glass back on the tray. Mom and Dad had been watching the exchange and had to have heard some of it. They were now beside us wanting to know what was going on.

While Jake explained, I realized my hands were still balled into fists. I relaxed them and wiggled my fingers. I couldn't believe that Victoria was the owner of that painting. I knew models sometimes made a lot of money, but that painting had to be worth at least a million. And I doubted that she bought it because she actually liked it. She wanted the prestige of owning a famous painting. She didn't care a whit about the painting itself. She'd lock it up and use it for bragging rights. I thought of the line from one of the Indiana Jones movies. To paraphrase Indy, *Face by Vermeer* belonged in a museum.

Lost in thought, I hadn't noticed Mom was talking to me and that Dad and Jake weren't there. "Sorry," I said. "I was thinking. Where did the guys go?"

Mom pointed to the food table. "Your father was hungry. He didn't have time to eat dinner." She touched my arm. "Are you okay? That had to be quite a shock."

"I'm fine. I never thought I'd actually get to meet the infamous Victoria." And I'd never wanted to.

Mom studied my face. "Jake loves you, you know."

I nodded. We hadn't actually made any declarations to each other, but we both knew that's what it was. "I know. And I know he's much happier now. I just hate what she did to him."

Jake and my dad returned with two plates full of various appetizers. I snatched a mini-quiche from Jake's plate.

"Hey! Hand's off, O'Hara," he said with a grin. I was relieved he was back to his usual self and that he wasn't going to let Victoria get the best of him. That wouldn't have been the case a few months ago.

We didn't stay much longer. We'd seen the painting, which was the reason we'd come. Although Victoria had looked our way several times, she'd been too busy with reporters and photographers to bother us again. We didn't even get to talk to Philip, but we did ask Marcus to tell him we said good-bye.

Jake was quiet on the short walk to the parking garage.

Once we were in his truck, he turned to me. "I hope you know that I'm over her."

"Of course I do." But it was nice to hear it.

He reached over and traced his finger down my cheek. "You're the one I care about. You're the best thing that ever happened to me."

"The feeling is mutual." I took his other hand in mine. "I will never do what she did to you and try to mold you into something you're not."

"I know you won't." He leaned over and kissed me.

It was a long kiss that seemed to go on forever and we were both breathless when we separated. "Wow," I said.

"Yeah." He took a deep breath and started the truck. "I'd better get you home before we steam up the windows."

I grinned. "You have defrosters in this thing, don't you?"

He laughed and put the truck in gear. "Yeah. But do you really want to make out in a truck in a parking garage?"

"I don't know. I've never done it before."

Jake shook his head. "This is no time to live dangerously, O'Hara."

"Spoilsport."

The good-natured teasing took the heat level in the truck down a notch. By the time we reached my loft building, my heartbeat had returned to normal. He walked me to my door and we said good night. I went in still thinking about that kiss.

I was up early the next morning and at the brewery by six. The hefeweizen was ready to keg, so I spent a couple of hours taking care of that and cleaning up. By the time I'd finished, my stomach was growling so I headed next door to the bakery.

Candy was behind the counter with her part-time weekend clerk. Everyone in Lawrenceville seemed to be hunting for sweets again this morning, and it was ten minutes before I made it to the front of the line.

"I'm sorry," Candy said. "Your chocolate muffins are all gone. And so are the apple cinnamon."

"That's okay. I'm in the mood for something different anyway." I quickly studied the contents in the case. "How about that blueberry muffin? I haven't had one of those in a while."

"It's all yours." She put it in a waxed bag and moved over to the cash register. "We're still on for Hartwood Acres tonight, aren't we?"

I nodded. "I really don't like you going." If there was some way I could talk her out of it, I would, but I knew it would be fruitless.

"I'll be fine," she assured me. You'll all be there and so will Tommy. Nothing is going to happen."

"I hope you're right." I paid for my muffin and she handed me the bag. "If you get a chance, stop over later. I have something big to tell you."

Candy's face broke out into a huge smile and she clapped her hands together. "Oh! Jake popped the question, didn't he? This is so exciting!"

My face turned redder than the T-shirt I was wearing. I'd better set her straight. And fast. "No, he didn't. It's nothing like that at all."

"Don't do that to me, Max. I don't know what that boy is waiting for. I've a mind to have a little talk with him."

"Don't you dare! Jake and I care about each other, but neither one of us is ready for that step yet. When—or if—the time comes, you'll be the first to know. After my mother, of course."

"I can't imagine what you want to tell me then."

I grinned. Time to give her a taste of her own medicine. "You'll just have to wait and see, won't you?" Before she could interrogate me and wrangle it out of me, I hurried out the door and jaywalked across the street to Jump, Jive & Java.

I pulled on the door at the same time someone pushed it from the inside and I almost went flying.

"Well, if it isn't Miss O'Hara." It was my former nemesis and my dad's partner, Detective Vincent Falk. Even on a Saturday morning, he was impeccably dressed as if he'd just stepped off the cover of *GQ*. He even smiled, which was an odd thing to see. Two months ago he'd wanted to haul Jake and me off to jail. He had been certain that Jake had poisoned the infamous food critic, Reginald Mobley, and I was his accomplice. He had gone to great lengths to prove it. He'd been wrong and had humbly admitted that fact. We'd called a truce since then.

"Good morning, Detective. What brings you to the neighborhood?"

"I stopped in to see a friend. I hear you found another body."

"You're not going to accuse me of murder again, are you?"

"Not this time," he said.

When he didn't ask who it was, I volunteered the infor-

mation. "The victim was a member of the band I hired for
Oktoberfest next weekend." I waited to see if he'd say anything about what he might have heard from Mitch. He didn't,
so I asked him if he knew if there were any suspects.

"I don't know anything, and even if I did, you know I
wouldn't be able to tell you."

I shrugged. "It was worth a try."

Vince reached into his pocket and pulled out his car keys.
"I have to run. Try and stay out of trouble."

When I went inside, the coffee shop was empty except
for Kristie. She was humming along to "It's Been a Long,
Long Time," the song that was playing on her sound system.
I'd never heard her do that before. She greeted me with a
huge smile. "Isn't it a beautiful day?" she said.

I suddenly put two and two together. Her recent hairstyle
change. The new man in her life she'd been trying to keep
secret. The humming. The smile. Vince Falk saying he'd
stopped in to see a friend. I smiled back at Kristie. "Why
didn't you tell me you were seeing Vince?"

The look of surprise on her face was priceless. Then she
laughed. "I should have known you'd figure it out, Miss
Detective."

"If Candy wasn't so preoccupied, I'm sure she would
have beat me to it."

"No doubt." Without asking, Kristie began making
my iced mocha. "I didn't want to say anything at first because I knew the two of you weren't all that fond of each
other."

"We've called a truce," I told her. "I still don't think he

likes me very much, but I can live with that. So how long has this been going on? Is it serious?"

"Not long. It's too soon to know how serious it is." Kristie handed me my drink and followed me to our usual table. "I didn't even like him at first. He talked to me after that food critic was killed—he had all kinds of questions about you and Jake." She smiled. "I told him off in no uncertain terms. I'm pretty sure his ears were ringing for hours."

I laughed. "I would have loved to have seen that."

"Yeah, it was one of my better moments. Anyway, after things settled down, he came in for coffee one morning and apologized. He said he wanted to make it up to me by buying me dinner. You know me—I'm not going to turn down a free meal."

"You must have made quite an impression on him. No one else got a free meal. I don't even think anyone else got an apology."

Kristie leaned forward, her elbows on the table. "I know you won't believe this, but he's the sweetest and funniest guy I've ever met."

I couldn't imagine it. "Are you sure we're talking about the same person? Rigid, opinionated, stiffly starched Vincent Falk?"

"One and the same."

I studied her face. She was head over heels for the guy. "I'll have to take your word for it, I guess. Now that your secret is out, you should bring him into the pub some night."

We chatted more while I finished my mocha. Before I left, I told her about going to Doodle's funeral and about the plan to go to Hartwood Acres tonight. "Are you up for it? Or do you have something else to do?"

"Vincent is working on some kind of task force thing, so I have no plans," Kristie said. "This is going to be fun."

"I don't know about fun, but it will definitely be interesting."

CHAPTER THIRTEEN

It was lunchtime before Candy came into the brew house. Nicole and I were behind the bar, and Candy sat on one of the stools eating Jake's semi-famous Buffalo chicken pierogies, while I told them about the gallery opening last night. When I got to the part about Victoria being there and that she was the buyer of the painting, Nicole audibly gasped.

"You're kidding," she said.

"Nope."

"I'm sure that went over well with Jake," Candy said. She knew all about his former fiancée. "What's the witch like?"

"Exactly how I imagined she'd be. Gorgeous and thin, with the personality of a snake. Although that might be giving snakes a bad name. I have a feeling she only bought that painting so she could say she owns something by a famous artist."

Cassie, one of the servers, came to the bar with a beer order and I poured it, then continued. "Jake made it clear he didn't want to have anything to do with her. I'm hoping by now she's on her way back to New York."

I looked up when the door opened. The infamous Victoria sashayed into the pub, followed by Philip Rittenhouse. Great. So much for hoping she'd be gone. I kind of felt sorry for Philip. Apparently he was at her beck and call. "Guess who just came in?" I said.

Nicole's eyes widened. "That's her?"

"The one and only." I didn't want to, but I went around the bar and headed their way.

Candy was right behind me. "Oh, this is going to be good."

I could only imagine what she was going to do. "Try and behave yourself." That was like asking a shark not to take a bite out of a tasty swimmer.

From the way Victoria was standing, it looked like she was trying to get the attention of everyone in the room. A few people glanced up, but most were too busy with their food. I reached her in seconds, with Candy right at my elbow.

I pasted a smile on my face, wishing I was wearing something besides the jeans and T-shirt that I'd worn that morning to keg beer. I probably smelled like it, too. At least I'd donned a clean apron. "Welcome to the Allegheny Brew House," I said.

I'd heard the expression *look down your nose at someone* numerous times, but this was the first time I'd actually seen anyone do it.

"Hello, Max," Victoria said. She swept her right arm over her head. "So this is your brewpub."

"Yes, it is."

"It's very quaint." She didn't say it like that was a good thing.

Candy nudged me aside, grabbed her hand, and pumped it like she was trying to shake bugs off it. "Oh. My. Gawd. I can't believe I'm meeting a supermodel. I see your picture in the fashion magazines and . . . oh, I just can't believe it!"

Philip took a step back in case he was next in Candy's line of attack.

Victoria's shocked expression changed to a smile. "Why, thank you very much. You don't know how much that means to me. To be recognized for my hard work is all that I ever ask for."

I could have gagged.

"Max was just telling me how you bought that old painting," Candy said. "What a wonderful thing to do. I imagine every museum in the world is going to want to display it."

"Um." Victoria's smile faltered. "I don't . . ."

Candy went on. "Some people would lock that painting up in a vault, but I can tell just to look at you, that you would want to share it with everyone. You seem like such a generous person."

If I'd have turned around, I was sure I'd have seen Nicole rolling her eyes.

"I can see it now—the famous painting hanging in a special exhibit with your name—in big letters, of course—right next to it," Candy said.

Victoria's smile returned. She was warming up to the idea. I could almost see the wheels turning in her head.

"You will be as famous as that painting's going to be." Candy beamed.

"That's exactly what I'm planning to do," Victoria said.

Philip had a puzzled expression on his face. "Are you sure? That's not what you said earlier."

"You must have misunderstood me, Philip. I want everyone to enjoy that painting as much as I do."

"I'm very glad about that. It would be a shame for a Vermeer to only be used as an investment," Philip said pointedly.

Touché.

"I'm going to call the Met first thing in the morning and set something up." She finally extricated her hand from Candy's and said to Philip, "I'll leave the painting with you until then, and you can have it shipped to me." She turned to me. "Would you mind finding us a table?" She gave me a catty smile. "I really miss Jake cooking for me."

$\mathfrak{I}$ made it through the lunch hour and Victoria's visit without throttling her although I'd been tempted more than once. I even convinced Jake to come out of the kitchen and talk to her. I told him the sooner he did, the sooner she'd leave. I went to my office and stayed there until Nicole let me know the coast was clear. I smiled to myself every time I thought about Candy's performance. She could have a third career as an actress if she wanted to.

The rest of the afternoon seemed to drag, although we were busy. I was anxious for tonight's . . . well, I wasn't sure what to call it. *Adventure* wasn't exactly the right word. Nicole had assured me she didn't mind working a little overtime and staying until the pub closed.

The Deutschmen were slated to perform at seven thirty, so I headed home at five thirty to get ready and take care of Hops. As much as I'd liked dressing up last night, I was glad I didn't have to do it again. It would be jeans and a sweater tonight. It had been warm all day, but in the last hour clouds had moved in and the temperature dropped a few degrees. I hoped the rain would hold off until after the evening's events.

Hops wasn't happy that I was going out again. She latched herself on to my pant leg and I had to peel her off. I told her we'd spend the day together tomorrow but she wasn't buying it. I finally tossed a few treats into her newly acquired shoe box bed and dashed out.

I was picking up Kristie and Daisy, and Jake was getting Elmer. We were all planning to meet up with Candy and Tommy in the parking lot off Middle Road, which was the designated lot for the amphitheater.

Hartwood Acres was one of several Allegheny County Parks and was located north of the city. It had been the estate of John and Mary Flinn Lawrence until 1969, when Mary sold the property to the county with the stipulation that she could remain there until her death, and that the county would not subdivide or sell the land for development. In addition to the amphitheater, there were numerous hiking and horse riding trails. The big draw, however, was the thirty-one-room Tudor-style stone mansion. It was open for tours and available for special events. It was often a location for bridal showers and receptions. There were a lot of wedding albums containing photos of the bride and groom with the mansion in the background.

I expected the parking lot to be full when we reached it but there were still half a dozen spots, plus the overflow area. I imagined many people had gone earlier in the day when the petting zoo and other activities for children were going on. Either that, or the clouds that were getting darker hour by hour were scaring people away.

Jake and Elmer had arrived before us and were standing beside Jake's truck. The three of us got out of my car and crossed the lot. Jake nudged Elmer. "Looks like we have the hottest dates in town."

Elmer grinned. "No doubt about that."

I gave Jake a kiss and Elmer a hug.

"I hear your ex is in town," Kristie said to Jake.

"And Candy had a little fun with her," Daisy added. "I really wish I could have seen that."

Elmer said, "That would have been a sight to behold. No stickly New York gal can hold a candle to any of yinz."

Daisy smiled. "Why, Elmer, did you just say something nice? That's twice in five minutes."

He winked. "Don't let that get around. I wouldn't want to ruin my reputation."

Just then, Candy pulled her gold sedan into the lot and squealed into a parking space. If Tommy didn't have whiplash after she slammed on the brakes, I'd be surprised. He was a little pale when he got out of the car and headed our way. He'd dropped his usual British-looking attire and adopted what could only be called *Pittsburgh Tourist*. Candy must have had something to do with that. I doubted that Tommy would have chosen any of it himself. He wore beige Bermuda shorts, a Pirates T-shirt with an unbuttoned Hawaiian shirt on top, and a Steelers ball cap. The best, however, were the sandals worn with black socks.

Candy looked like her usual black and gold self. They were a perfect couple.

"I hardly recognized you, Tommy," I said.

"I look ridiculous, I know," he said. "Candace insisted I wear this getup."

"Of course I did. You're supposed to be undercover and look like a tourist."

"I could have been a dignified tourist. Instead I look like . . . I'm not even sure what to call this."

"We talked about this. Josef would recognize you in an instant if you dressed like you usually do," she said.

"What's your excuse, then?" Elmer asked. "You don't look any different."

Candy rolled her eyes. "No kidding. If I looked different, Josef would be sure to suspect something. He's already seen me and knows this is how I dress."

I was a little puzzled. "I thought you wanted him to recognize both of you."

"Change of plans," Candy said. "If Josef doesn't realize this is Tommy, he might be more likely to approach me."

After a brief discussion, we decided that Jake and I would head for the amphitheater first since I'd already told Felix we were going to be there. A few minutes later, Elmer, Kristie, and Daisy would follow. Candy and Tommy would come in last—after the band began playing. Now that we were here, I realized it wasn't much of a plan. Even if Felix approached Candy and Tommy, he wasn't going to admit he'd killed Doodle. And unless he could get Candy or Tommy alone, it would be difficult for him to try anything with so many people around. At least I hoped that was the case.

I voiced my concerns to Jake while we walked. "I'm not sure this is going to accomplish anything."

"It's worth a try. It's probably the best way to talk to Felix without him suspecting anything."

We arrived at the amphitheater area in no time at all. Hundreds of people had gathered on the lawn in front of the stage. Some had spread blankets on the ground, and others lounged in lawn chairs. More than a few had picnic baskets, which was a great idea. We'd have to come back next summer for a concert and make it into a picnic.

The Deutschmen wouldn't take the stage for another thirty minutes, so Jake and I strolled toward the rear of the stage. We found Bruce, Manny, and Felix unloading sound equipment from a white van.

"Need some help?" Jake asked.

Manny grinned. "All we can get."

I introduced Jake and we helped them lug their equipment onto the stage. When I lifted a thirty-pound speaker like it was nothing, Felix looked surprised. I smiled at him. "I'm stronger than I look. I'm used to hauling fifty-pound bags of malt around."

When we'd finished, Bruce clapped Jake on the back.

"Thanks, man." He shook my hand. "I appreciate the help. At the very least we owe you two a drink."

We told them we were happy to help and we'd see them after the show. I hoped our assisting them would leave them open to answering a few questions later. I was a step ahead of Jake when we rounded the stage and ran right into Paisley.

"Oh!" she said. "I'm so sorry. I didn't see you."

"I'm sorry, too," I said. "I didn't see you, either."

Paisley studied my face. "Weren't you at my brother's funeral?"

"Yes, I was. I'm Max O'Hara."

"That's right," she said. "I'm not so good with names but I never forget a face."

I introduced her to Jake.

"My sister and I are here to watch the band. They were good friends to Walter and I wanted to come and support them."

As surprised as I was that Paisley was here, I was even more so that Rhonda had come. This didn't seem like her kind of event. It might be a good opportunity to find out more about her brother and the other band members.

Jake must have been thinking the same thing because he asked Paisley if she and her sister would like to hang out with us and listen to the band.

Paisley gave him a big smile. "I would love to, but I'm not sure about Rhonda. She said something about sitting backstage, but I'll ask her. She wanted to see the mansion first."

We moved off to the side of the stage, where we wouldn't

block anyone's view. I spotted Kristie, Daisy, and Elmer and waved my arms until they saw me. When they reached us, I introduced them to Paisley.

"Interesting name you've got there, young lady," Elmer said.

"Thank you," she said. "My parents didn't know what to name me and the first thing my mother saw was her paisley scarf she'd worn to the hospital, and she thought that would be a lovely name."

Paisley looked away, and Elmer caught my eye and mouthed "Nutso" to me.

"It's a beautiful name," Daisy said.

When the music began a minute later, Paisley said she was going to look for her sister and she'd be back. The rest of us turned toward the stage. I saw Candy and Tommy standing on the lawn at the other corner of the stage. If Felix looked that way, he'd surely see them. I nudged Jake and pointed. "Over there."

"I see them," he said.

Throughout the band's set, my gaze kept going back and forth between the stage and Candy. The Deutschmen's repertoire was more varied than what they'd played at the fire hall party. In between polkas and German songs, they played and sang some oldies and classic rock. Apparently Bruce Hoffman's keyboard was a multipurpose instrument that even simulated guitar and drumbeats.

The three remaining band members took turns introducing songs. When they'd been performing about forty-five minutes, it was Felix's turn. "This will be the last song in this set, then we're going to take a little break and be back in a bit. When this song first came out, the world was a different place. It was all so complicated back then. We questioned everything and didn't trust anyone. The world is not any simpler now, but I think we've learned a few things over the years. At least I have." He cleared his throat. "Before I bore you any further, I'll end with saying I'd like to dedicate this song to a very old friend." He turned his head toward the spot where Candy and Tommy were. "Her name was Catherine."

CHAPTER FOURTEEN

The band launched into an old Elvis Presley tune, "Suspicious Minds." Even from the opposite end of the stage, I could see Candy's face pale. Tommy put his arm around her. "That's for Candy," I said. "Felix must have known her as Catherine." I didn't wait for anyone's comments. I spun around and headed behind the stage and over to the other side. I heard Daisy ask where I was going. I didn't stop to answer.

Candy had recovered by the time I reached them and she was arguing with Tommy. "I am not leaving," she said. "Not until I know more."

Tommy was having none of that. "You wanted him to see you. He did and he most certainly remembers who you are. Don't tell me you don't remember the proper procedure—once you're compromised, you get out."

"I don't give a rat's patootie about any proper procedure. I'm a civilian now and can do things my way, which in retrospect would have worked out a whole lot better. Following protocol is what got us into trouble in the first place."

"We didn't have a choice," he said.

"Yes, we did. If we would have confronted Josef in the first place instead of running away—"

"We would both be dead," Tommy said. "Don't forget—there were eyes and ears everywhere."

Candy crossed her arms. "I am staying and that's all there is to it. If you want to leave, go right ahead. It's not like you haven't done it before."

Ouch.

Tommy turned to me. "Talk some sense into her, Max. She won't listen to me."

I nodded my head toward the stage. "Instead of the two of you bickering, you should think about what you're going to do when the song is over. I was dead set against both of you coming here in the first place, but since you have, you might as well make the best of it."

I couldn't believe I'd just said that and neither could Candy. She had opened her mouth to likely give me a reason she wasn't leaving, but closed it again. Just then there was a loud clap of thunder followed by a flash of lightning. The band stopped playing and Bruce Hoffman announced that for safety reasons the concert was over. Before I had a chance to even process that, the clouds opened up and the rain that had been threatening for hours finally came.

People in the crowd hurriedly gathered up their belongings and dashed for the parking lot or whatever cover they could find. Candy, Tommy, and I ran for the stage since we were so close to it. Jake and the others did the same from the opposite side.

The band members were center stage, beginning to gather up their equipment. Felix was slipping his accordion strap over his head and paused when he saw us, then removed it and placed it in the case. Candy and Tommy stopped at the edge of the stage.

"Are you sure you want to do this, love?" Tommy asked her.

"I am."

I thought Felix would head our way, but instead he snapped his accordion case closed, said something to Bruce, went down the rear steps of the stage, and ran for his car. I hadn't expected that. Candy and I looked at each other and it was apparent she hadn't, either.

"That was interesting," Tommy said. "I believe you frightened him away, my dear."

While we waited for the rain to stop, Jake and I helped Bruce and Manny pack up the rest of their stuff. When Elmer began complaining that he didn't have anything to do, I gave my car keys to Daisy to take him home. Kristie went with her. I told her to leave the keys with Nicole at the pub and I'd have Jake drop me off later to pick up the car. Candy and Tommy stuck around and asked a few questions about Felix, until Manny asked them why they were asking so many questions. Candy made up a story that wasn't too far from the truth. She told them that Felix really had recognized her last week and that he was an old friend she hadn't seen in many years.

It wasn't until we'd finished that Paisley came back with her sister. Rhonda was dressed more informally than she'd been at the funeral, but her navy slacks and navy and white striped jersey still looked expensive. Even though the rain was just a drizzle by then, the sisters were under a white golf umbrella that Rhonda carried. She closed it and handed it to Paisley.

Rhonda's gaze went from one person to another and finally rested on me. "Weren't you at Walter's funeral?" she said.

Paisley answered for me. "Yes, she was. And don't be mean to her. She's been very nice to me."

"Fine. Whatever." Rhonda spun around and walked to where Bruce was loading the van.

He greeted her with an embrace that seemed much more than a casual one. The way she leaned into him and touched his arm while they talked made me wonder if they were lovers.

Paisley noticed I was watching them. "They make an interesting couple, don't they?" she said. "They've been seeing each other for a while now. Walter wasn't crazy about it."

"Why not?" I asked.

"He said they were too much alike. I don't think that's a bad thing, do you?" She didn't wait for an answer. "I told him he should be happy. If it wasn't for them, Walter wouldn't have sold any of the things he'd been working on. I'm going to talk to Manny. See you later." She flitted across the stage.

Jake put his arm around me. "Ready to go?"

"Definitely." We hollered a good-bye to Bruce and Manny, and along with Candy and Tommy, headed to the parking lot.

Daisy had left my car safe and sound in the lot beside the pub. Jake had gone home after dropping me off because he was scheduled to assist with the high school hockey practice again at the ridiculous hour of four a.m. I'd planned to meet with Candy and Tommy at her house once I got my car, so I promised to fill Jake in at Sunday dinner. I made a quick trip inside to get my keys. It was a typical busy Saturday night, and I stopped briefly to chat with a few regulars before leaving again.

Candy lived in a quaint row house on a side street only a few blocks from Cupcakes N'at. She'd bought the house back when the neighborhood had been considered distressed. One by one, the houses had been sold and renovated, and likely tripled in value. Most of her neighbors were now up and coming professionals who preferred city living to the suburbs.

Tommy answered the door when I arrived. He'd ditched the Hawaiian shirt and had traded the black socks and sandals for bedroom slippers. "Come in, my dear. Candace will be down momentarily. She's upstairs changing."

I followed him down a hallway that went past the living room and into Candy's neat kitchen.

"I took the liberty of making tea," he said. "Unless you prefer something stronger."

"Tea is perfect. Thank you." I sat down at the small

tile-topped table. When Candy had found the table at a flea market, it hadn't been in the greatest shape. She had taken it home and a week later had me stop by to see it. She'd removed the plain white cracked tile and replaced it with colorful mosaic. She had painted and antiqued the rest of it. It turned out beautifully.

Tommy poured tea into a cup and handed it to me. "Before Candace comes down, I want to thank you for being such a good friend to her, especially over the past week. It's been very stressful for her. It took her years to come to terms with shooting Josef and she thought it was all in the past."

"Candy's been a good friend to me as well. I haven't done anything that she hasn't done for me a thousand times over. I just wish she wouldn't have kept this all to herself."

He smiled. "You know Candace."

I returned the smile. "Yes, I do."

Candy came into the kitchen just then. She had changed into pink pajamas, a terry cloth robe, and pink bunny slippers. It was odd seeing her in a different color. "Nice slippers," I said.

"Thanks." She sat down beside Tommy on the other side of the table and poured a cup of tea for herself. "I don't know what to make of tonight."

"I don't either," I said. "Why would Felix leave after practically calling you out? It doesn't make sense."

"Maybe he thought I was going to shoot him again. If I ran into someone who'd shot me, I'd hightail it out of there, too. He probably expected me to run off when he called me 'Catherine.' That was the alias I used back then, by the way."

"He should have known you're not one to back down from a fight," I said.

Tommy refilled his cup. "He's biding his time for some reason. He wants whatever he has planned to be on his own schedule."

I sipped my tea. "But why? Why is he here? Did he already know Candy lived here, or did he only find out when we showed up at the Oktoberfest party? How and why did he get involved with the Deutschmen? Did Doodle really know something about Felix that got him killed?"

Candy smiled. "You certainly have a lot of questions."

"Good ones, too," Tommy added.

I asked, "So how do we get answers?"

Candy tapped her fingernails on the table while she thought about it, then pushed her teacup aside. "You said those two women were Doodle's sisters?"

I nodded. "Rhonda and Paisley."

"I think we should start with them."

Tommy agreed. "It's likely they know Felix better than anyone. If nothing else, they certainly knew their brother. It's possible something they say or do will lead us closer to discovering what Felix has in mind."

"I'm sure Rhonda knows Bruce pretty well." I told them what I'd witnessed right before we left Hartwood. "Rhonda is also a little snobby. I doubt she would tell us much."

"I'd talk to Paisley then," Candy said. "She seems like she'd be a little more forthcoming with information."

I agreed. "Paisley certainly likes to talk and it's possible she'd reveal a lot without even knowing she's doing it. I'll call her tomorrow and set something up. Do you want to come with me?"

"I'd love to," Candy said.

"Tommy?"

He shook his head. "I'll leave that to you ladies. In the meantime, I'm going to ring up my contacts again and see if they've made any progress in discovering what Josef has been doing all these years. They haven't had any information so far."

I finished my tea and Candy walked me to the door. "I'll let you know as soon as I get ahold of Paisley."

"Sounds good."

Halfway out the door I remembered something. "Did Mom call you about coming to dinner tomorrow?"

"She did. We'll be there." She suddenly crushed me to her in a bear hug. I usually dreaded these, but I didn't mind it so much this time. When she released me, she said, "Thanks for everything, Max. You are a dear, dear friend."

I nodded and headed to my car. I couldn't get any words out—they stuck in my throat. I blinked away the tears in my eyes. I hated seeing Candy like this. She'd always been larger than life. There had been moments over the past week when she'd been her old self, but that wasn't enough. I wanted the old Candy back. I vowed to do whatever I could to make that happen.

When I got home, I played with my neglected cat. Hops made sure I knew that I hadn't paid nearly enough attention to her over the last couple of days. When she finally tired of playing, she went to the bedroom and coiled up in her shoe box. It looked like that might be her permanent bed. This week anyway.

I was hungry so I fixed a bowl of cereal, which was about all I had in the kitchen other than peanut butter or cat food. When I'd finished, I rinsed the bowl and left it in the sink. After I got ready for bed, I was still wide awake, so I took my laptop to the living room and booted it up. It was time to ask my good friend Google for some information.

I began with the victim, Walter "Doodle" Dowdy. The first thing that came up was his obituary. I'd looked at it briefly the other day, but now read it again. It mentioned his sisters, Paisley Dowdy and Rhonda Dowdy Williams. Rhonda must have been married at some point. Either that, or she'd changed her name. There was nothing else of interest so I moved on.

The next entry was a newspaper article from a year ago about the Deutschmen. Felix hadn't joined the group as yet. The fourth member back then was a Roy Williams—the same last name as Rhonda. Now that was an interesting tidbit. If Roy had been her husband, had Bruce Hoffman come between them? I opened a new tab and Googled *Roy Williams Pittsburgh*. There were too many hits so I added *Deutschmen* to the search. The only things that came up were some old listings of appearances and the article I'd been reading. I'd add Roy to my list of questions for Paisley.

I went back to Doodle's search and scrolled through another Google page, then clicked through to the next. At the top of page two, there was a website link for *Walter Dowdy, Artist*. I vaguely remembered seeing a couple of canvases and some art supplies in Doodle's house, but no paintings.

I was pleasantly surprised when I clicked on the link and saw photos of his paintings on the website. Most of them were landscapes. Some of them looked familiar, like I'd seen them before. A few others were clearly scenes of Pittsburgh. There were several portraits of people painted in different styles—some old-fashioned, some modern. There was even one of his sisters. Although these were photos and not the actual paintings, he was clearly very talented.

His site had a rather noninteresting bio and a page where you could buy the featured paintings. The last tab at the top of the page read *Commissioned Works*. When I clicked on the tab, it asked for a password. Weird. I tried it again with the same result. Another thing to add to my questions for Paisley.

Next, I typed *Bruce Hoffman* and *Pittsburgh* into the search bar. Everything that came up had to do with the band. I tried *Manny Levin* and got the same thing. Finally, I entered *Felix Holt* and got the same result.

I shouldn't have been disappointed, but I was. After all, Tommy's contacts hadn't come up with anything yet so I shouldn't have expected an Internet search to turn up something that government agencies couldn't find. To disappoint myself further, I tried *Josef Bartek* and got absolutely nothing.

Before I logged off for the night, I decided to check my e-mail and there was one from Mom.

Hi Sweetie. Philip sent me some photos from the gallery opening and there are some good ones of you and Jake. There are some of the four of us as well. I've attached them. See you tomorrow.

Hopefully, Victoria wasn't in any of them. I opened the attachment. She was right—they were great photos. There was one of Mom, Dad, Jake, and me that I especially liked. It would be great to get printed and framed, which reminded me that I should take the photo of the blessing of the barrels that Fran had given me to Sunday dinner to show Sean. When I got to the last photo, someone in the background caught my eye. Figuring I was seeing things, I enlarged the photo. It hadn't been my imagination at all.

Felix Holt had been at the gallery opening.

CHAPTER FIFTEEN

What in the world had Felix been doing at the gallery? I studied the photo closely. He stood just inside the door. He wore a nice suit so he blended in with the other men who either wore suits or tuxedos. Why hadn't I seen him there? And if he saw me, why didn't he stop and say hello? Had he been in any other photos? Too many questions and no answers.

I wondered if Philip had more photos. Mom had attached these instead of forwarding whatever he had sent her. One way to find out. I replied to Mom's e-mail thanking her for sending the pictures and asked if Philip had sent more—that I wouldn't mind seeing all of them. I also asked for Philip's e-mail address. If he hadn't sent other photos to her, I could then ask him directly.

As much as I wanted to wait for a reply from my mother, I closed my laptop and placed it on the kitchen counter. It was after eleven p.m. and I doubted very much she was still awake. I'd check it in the morning before I left for Mass. I headed for bed.

The first thing I did when I woke up at six—after feeding Hops, of course, who let me know in no uncertain terms that she was starving—was check my e-mail. Mom was an early riser so I wasn't surprised to see she'd sent a response an hour ago. She had forwarded Philip's e-mail, which contained photos in a zip file instead of the half-dozen she'd chosen for me. Mom closed the e-mail with the warning that some of the photos included Victoria. I smiled to myself, figuring that was why she hadn't forwarded Philip's e-mail in the first place. Maybe I could have one of Victoria's photos enlarged to hang on the dartboard in the pub.

While the zip file downloaded and opened, I made a cup of coffee with my new machine. I only made coffee at home a few days a week, so when my old four-cup coffeemaker bit the dust, I opted for a single-serve one. I was still getting used to it, but so far I liked getting an almost instantaneous cup of java. I added my usual milk and sugar and sat down at the kitchen counter.

There were fifty photos in all. I flipped through them quickly then went back to the beginning to study them closely. A dozen of them featured Victoria—smiling, posing beside the painting, hanging on Philip's arm, and a few with local celebrities. She definitely loved the limelight. I studied the background in her photos, but they were so focused on her that everything else was completely blurred.

I did find Felix in a few more photos. He was in the midst of a crowd in all but one. In that one, he was bent over with his face only a few inches from the painting. Other than that, nothing stood out to me. If I hadn't known so much about him from Candy, I wouldn't think anything of seeing him there, other than he was an art lover. And maybe that's all it was. Just because he'd been a spy didn't mean he couldn't be a patron of the arts. He was a musician, after all. Art and music kind of went together.

By the time I'd finished going through the photos, it was almost seven thirty—too late to make the eight o'clock Mass at the local church. But I could make the nine at Most Holy Name. I'd not only make my weekly obligation, I'd make my brother Sean very happy.

As it turned out, a visiting priest had the nine o'clock Mass so I wouldn't get to see my oldest brother until that afternoon. On the way back home, I grabbed a breakfast sandwich from a drive-thru. I made another cup of coffee, and while I ate, I looked up Paisley's number. I gave the last bit of my sandwich to Hops, then made the call.

She answered on the third ring. I identified myself and asked her if she had a minute.

"Of course I do," she said. "I'm glad you called. I wanted to thank you for being so helpful last night. And so friendly. I don't have many friends."

"I find that hard to believe."

"Well, it's true."

I launched into my request. "I was wondering if you had some free time today or tomorrow." I expected her to ask me why but she didn't.

"I do," she said. "I would love to get together with you. How about tomorrow morning? We could do breakfast."

"Perfect." I suggested the same Eat'n Park where Jake and I had gone. It wouldn't be far for either of us.

"Wonderful!"

"Do you mind if my friend Candy comes, too?"

"Not at all. This will be so much fun!"

I felt a little guilty that she had gotten the wrong impression but it was too late to fix it now. We made arrangements to meet at nine and said good-bye. Hopefully Candy could make that work.

Candy was my next call. I told her about Paisley and asked if she'd be able to make it for breakfast.

"I should be able to get away," she said. "The morning rush should be just about over, and Mary Louise can handle it."

I told her about the pictures Mom had forwarded.

"Are you sure it was him?" she asked.

"Yes. It was definitely Felix. I'll bring my laptop this afternoon and you can see for yourself."

"Now that I think about it," Candy said, "it wasn't one of his official duties, but Josef was very interested in antiquities and art. He may have mentioned once that his field of study had been in that area."

"That explains his interest in the Vermeer."

"I remember him yelling at a man because a painting

was hanging upside down. I didn't blame the guy. It was one of those modern things, and to me it looked the same no matter which way you turned it."

After that, I talked briefly with Jake and he said he'd meet me at my parents' house later. I had some time yet, so I straightened up the apartment a bit and threw a load of wash in. One of the best things about this place was that there was no communal laundry room. I had my very own stacked washer and dryer hidden away in a closet beside the bathroom. Now all I had to do was remember to put the wash in the dryer when I got home later.

I packed up Hops and her belongings, grabbed my laptop, and headed out. We made a quick stop at the brew house to fill a few growlers and grab Fran's photo, then it was on to Mom and Dad's.

I was the first family member to arrive, which meant I would get to spend some quality time with my mom. At least that's what I thought until I saw the backyard. It was a veritable cop convention. Dad was on the patio with his old partner Rich Bailey, who had retired a few months ago, Mitch Raines, and the biggest surprise of all—Vincent Falk. "What's up with that?" I asked Mom as I set the growlers on the kitchen counter on my second trip into the house. I'd brought Hops and my laptop in first, then went out to my car to retrieve three growlers.

"I'm not quite sure. Rich was in town and stopped by, and before I knew it, the other two were here. I suppose either your dad or Rich let them know."

"I hope I brought enough beer."

Mom smiled. "It will have to be enough. Why don't you take it out and put it in the cooler."

I carried the growlers out to the patio. "I guess you guys were waiting for these."

Rich stood and opened the cooler. "You raised this girl right, Sean."

The others laughed—even Vince. That was something that would be hard to get used to. I gave Dad a hug, and greeted Mitch and Vince. I handed Rich a brown ale and a lager to put in the cooler, then opened the hefeweizen. Dad had glasses ready, so I poured and he passed them around.

Mitch tasted the beer. "You made this, Max? It's really good."

"Don't sound so surprised," I said with a smile.

"I didn't mean it that way," he said. "I tried homebrewing a couple times and the results were . . . well . . . less than satisfactory. It's hard work."

"Nice save," Vince said.

I couldn't resist. I had to say it. "Have you switched bodies with someone with a personality?"

Mitch snorted and Rich said, "Guess she told you." Dad just raised an eyebrow.

Vince laughed. He actually laughed. "Touché, Miss O'Hara."

"You know you can call me Max."

"I'll try to remember that."

I went inside to see if Mom needed help, and she sent me back out with chips and pretzels. I noticed Mitch was on the other side of the yard checking out Dad's grill. I put the snacks down on the glass-topped table and headed that way. "Mind if I ask you a few questions?"

"Ask away," he said. "I'll answer them if I can."

No sense beating around the bush. "How is the investigation going?"

He grinned. "What investigation might that be? I'm working on several."

"Very funny. You know which one."

"There's nothing new," he said. "We haven't ruled anything out, but there haven't been any new leads. Nothing has panned out yet. We've interviewed friends, family, you name it. We're starting to lean toward a break-in that went wrong."

"Seriously?" I was disappointed and I guess it showed on my face.

"I'm sorry I don't have better news," Mitch said.

I was about to tell him that I didn't believe for one minute that Doodle had been killed because he'd been at the wrong place at the wrong time, when Mike came outside carrying a football. Jake and Sean were right behind him. Our conversation was over. The Sunday game was about to begin.

I didn't get to talk to Mitch again. He left right after the football game. Dad and Rich didn't play, choosing to sit and catch up before Rich went back to North Carolina. Candy and Tommy arrived just as the game ended.

"Don't tell me I missed it," Candy said. "I even brought my Terrible Towel." She swirled the gold towel like any hardcore Steelers fan would.

Jake reached for it. "I'm a little sweaty. Can I borrow that?"

Candy whipped it behind her back. "Don't even think about it."

I noticed Vince stayed far away from my friend. He'd been subject to one of her bear hugs in the past, and I think he was still afraid of her. I caught his eye and smiled. I introduced Tommy to everyone, and he soon seemed right at home.

It wasn't until after dinner that I had a chance to show the photos to Candy. My sister-in-law Kate was helping Mom clean up. They assured me they didn't need my help so Candy and I went to the living room, where my nieces were watching a Disney movie with Hops. Technically, Hops was sleeping, but Fiona, who had just turned three years old, insisted the cat loved the movie.

Candy and I sat on the couch, and I opened the laptop and switched it on. Fiona's older sister, Maire, who would be five in December, alternated her gaze between the TV and Candy. After a minute or so, she got up off the floor, came over to the couch, and stared at Candy.

"Do you need something, Maire?" I asked.

Instead of answering me, she said to Candy, "Are you here to see if we're being good?"

I couldn't help smiling. I knew where this was going.

"Why would you ask that?" Candy said.

"When we were at Aunt Max's restaurant for that big party, Daddy said we had to be good so you could tell Santa."

Candy glanced over at me and raised both eyebrows.

She took both of Maire's hands in hers. "Well, if your

daddy said that, it must be true. It seems to me you are both very good girls. I'll be sure to let Santa know. And I'll be sure to tell your daddy, too."

I stifled a laugh. Mike was in big trouble.

Candy's remarks seemed to put Maire at ease, and she went back to her seat on the floor.

"Your brother needs a good talking to," Candy said.

I shrugged. "You know Mike."

"I have a mind to tell those girls Santa will bring them lots and lots and lots of toys. And maybe a couple of those expensive American Girl dolls."

"You wouldn't!"

"Try me."

"Why don't we look at these instead?" I opened the photo file and moved my laptop to where we both could see it. The first one was a picture of Jake and me.

She leaned closer. "I like that! You should get that enlarged. And that one of you and your parents." She scrolled through more. "It looks like it was quite an event." She paused briefly on a couple of Victoria's photos but didn't comment. When she reached the one with Felix standing by the door at the back of the crowd, I pointed it out. She asked if I could make it bigger.

I clicked the enlarge button twice. "How's that?"

"Much better. That does look like Josef." She went to the next photo, which was the one where he was peering at the painting. "That's definitely him." She drummed her fingernails on her leg—a sure sign she was thinking. "Was this event open to the public, or by invitation only?"

"I think it was open, but I'm sure certain people like the politicians received invitations. Why?"

"If it was by invitation only, it would be easy to find out exactly why Josef was there."

"I can ask Philip."

Sean entered the living room just then. "There you are," he said. "I was wondering where you got to."

"I was showing Candy the photos from the gallery opening last night."

He sat down on the other side of me. "Can I see them? Mom said it was a great evening."

"Sure," I said. "But I have something else to show you first."

Candy got up. "I'm going to see what trouble Tommy has gotten into." On her way out of the room, she patted my nieces on their heads and whispered something to them that left them beaming. Mike was definitely in for it.

I reached into my bag on the floor and pulled out the framed photo Fran had given me. "You might like this." I passed it to Sean.

He smiled. "This is great! I know they used to bless the barrels, but I didn't realize they did any at my church. Where did you get this?"

He knew about the beer museum and he'd met Fran before. I told him she'd given it to me. "I'm going to hang it in the pub somewhere."

"And I'll be sure to send all my parishioners in to see it," Sean said.

"Good idea." I moved the laptop over so Sean could see and went back to the first photo.

"Wow," he said. "You clean up pretty well, Maxie."

"Thanks. I think." We went through the pictures, and when we got to the one with Felix looking at the painting, he stopped me.

"Hey, I know that guy." Sean pointed to the photo.

"Him? Are you sure?" I asked.

"I'm positive. That's Felix Holt."

CHAPTER SIXTEEN

"You know Felix?" I asked. I couldn't imagine how that was possible.

"Not well, but I've talked with him several times," Sean said. "He comes into the chapel a lot." He meant Saint Anthony's Chapel, which was part of Holy Name parish. "He's fascinated by the relics and he's particularly fond of the Stations." The chapel not only had the most relics of saints anywhere outside the Vatican, it contained life-size, hand-carved Stations of the Cross.

"I can't believe it. I can't believe you've actually talked to him."

Sean laughed. "Why not? I do get to talk to people on occasion."

"I know that."

"How do you know Felix Holt?" Sean asked.

"It's a long story." I put my laptop down and grabbed his hand. "Come with me. Candy needs to hear this." I practically dragged him out of the room.

"Do you want to tell me what's going on?" Sean asked as we headed down the hall and through the kitchen. "I'm really confused."

"I'll tell you in a minute." We'd reached the door to the patio by this time. Candy and Tommy were standing near Jake. She had her purse over her arm and it looked like she and Tommy were getting ready to leave. All three saw me and I motioned for them to come into the kitchen.

"What's going on?" Jake asked. "Is something wrong?"

"Everything's fine, but you're not going to believe this." I told them what Sean had just revealed.

Tommy said to Sean, "And he told you his name was Felix Holt?"

Sean nodded. "Why is everyone so interested in this guy?"

Candy looked at me. "You didn't tell him?"

"I figured it wasn't up to me. It's your story."

She patted Sean on the back. "Well then, you'd better have a seat. This could take a while."

The next morning at the brewery, I did my usual check of the gauges on the tanks, then sterilized barrels to keg the Oktoberfest beer. I thought about the Felix Holt situation while I worked. I still couldn't get over the fact that Sean knew him. It had taken Candy a good half hour to tell Sean about how she and Tommy knew Felix. If my brother had been shocked, he hadn't shown it, but I imagine in his line of work, he'd heard just about everything. He told Candy he'd pray for a good resolution for all concerned. I think she appreciated that.

At eight thirty, Candy and I got in my car and headed to Eat'n Park to meet Paisley Dowdy. I hoped she'd be able to shed a little light on some things. We were a few minutes early so we waited inside near the bakery case for Paisley. I tried not to drool at the Oreo Cream Pie staring me right in my face. I turned my back so I wouldn't be tempted to order a whole pie for breakfast.

Paisley arrived right on time. She smiled widely when she saw us. "I am so happy we could do this," she said. "I don't get out to breakfast very often. This will be so much fun!" She clapped her hands together.

Candy glanced at me and raised an eyebrow. She'd only met Paisley briefly at Hartwood Acres so this was the first time my friend had gotten the full effect. When the hostess led us to our seats, Paisley was ahead of us. Candy whispered to me, "If she starts skipping and singing to forest animals, I'm out of here."

I grinned. "What if she has a fairy godmother? Everyone could use one of those."

We sat across from Paisley, who chattered the whole time she was reading the menu. Candy nudged me with her knee at least a half-dozen times. Paisley finally decided to order the *Waffle Smile*, which was exactly what it sounded like—a waffle with a smiley face on one side of the waffle. I was more conservative and ordered a ham and cheese omelet with toast and home fries, and Candy opted for the breakfast burritos.

Before I even had a chance to figure out where to begin with the questions I had for Paisley, she said, "My brother loved burritos. Actually he loved any kind of spicy food. If he ordered eggs like you did Max, he'd put hot sauce all over them. Rhonda likes Italian food, but her husband—he's dead now—he liked sweets like I do." She paused to sip her tea.

That answered one of my unasked questions—who was Roy Williams and what happened to him? "I didn't realize your sister had been married," I said.

"Oh yes. Roy. I liked him a lot. Rhonda thought he was boring."

"Why was that?"

She shrugged. "I'm not really sure. It had something to do with Walter. They had a big fight about him and then Roy moved out."

I had expected her to say it was because of Bruce, not Doodle.

Paisley continued. "I tried to get Roy to come back but he said not until Rhonda came to her senses. And then there was that terrible accident and he was killed." She sighed.

Candy and I exchanged looks. "A car accident?" Candy asked.

"Oh, no. Someone broke into his apartment."

"And killed him?" Candy said.

"He fell down the stairs."

I wasn't following this very well. "In his apartment?"

Paisley shook her head. "Outside his apartment. The police said his apartment door was open when Roy got home and he probably surprised the burglar, who probably ran past him and probably bumped into Roy and he fell down the concrete stairs."

That was a lot of probablies.

"They never caught the person who broke in. Poor Roy."

"At least Rhonda has Bruce now," I said. "That has to be some comfort."

Paisley nodded. "It is. Bruce is nice enough, I guess. And he was a big help to Walter. My brother was an artist, you know."

Another opening. "Yes. I saw some of his work on his website. The painting he did of you and your sister looked exactly like you two."

"Thank you," she said. "I have that one hanging in my house. I should take you to see some of his paintings that are still at Rhonda's. He had a studio there, but he was beginning to move everything to his house after he finished fixing it up."

Candy and I looked at each other. We were thinking the same thing but couldn't very well tell Paisley that we'd been in his house and hadn't seen any paintings. Our food came then and discussion was temporarily halted. I practically inhaled everything on my plate.

Paisley was much slower, most likely because she talked in between bites. She continued to talk about her brother and how much he loved art and how much he loved playing in his band.

"How did Felix come to join the band?" Candy asked.

Paisley finally pushed her plate aside. "I'm not really sure. Bruce said Felix had been a friend of Roy's. They needed another accordion player so they hired him."

I wondered if Felix really had been a friend of Roy's or if it was a ruse. The more I heard about the whole situation, the more confused I was. None of this answered the question of why Felix was with the band in the first place. If he had come to town because Candy was here, why go through all this pretense? He would've had no idea I'd hire the Deutschmen. Six months ago I hadn't even known they existed. Was it possible he ended up in the same city as Candy by pure coincidence? If so, what else had I been wrong about?

ack at the brew house, I went into the brewery after the lunch rush to move the Oktoberfest beer from the fermenter to the kegs I'd sterilized earlier. I couldn't shake the feeling that I had it all wrong. If Felix wasn't here because of Candy, why was he here? How did a foreign former spy end up in Pittsburgh of all places? It wasn't exactly the hotbed of espionage.

I needed to reconsider what I knew and start over. I thought back to the night that Candy, Daisy, Kristie, and I had gone to the fire hall Oktoberfest party to see the Deutschmen. Felix only thought he might have known Candy from somewhere. He hadn't been sure. Candy recognized him, though. It must have hit him later who she was.

Then there was the phone call from Doodle. I tried to remember his exact words but couldn't. Did he even mention Felix? I couldn't remember for sure. Had I just imagined that part? I'd assumed an awful lot about that phone call. It seemed ridiculous now that I'd thought he wanted to fix Felix up with Candy.

The first keg began to spit beer out of the tubing so I closed it off and connected the tubing to the next barrel. So what had Doodle wanted to tell me? If it had involved Candy, it had to include Felix as well. There was no other explanation. He hadn't known Candy at all, but I had no way of knowing whether Doodle had somehow found out about their past connection.

Next, I'd found Candy in Doodle's house when I'd gone to meet him. She'd been trying to find out what he knew. Now that I knew about what had happened between Candy, Tommy, and Felix, I understood her panic at the thought that Felix had been out to get her. The more I learned about Felix, though, the less I thought that was why he was here. He would have made a move on her by now.

My thoughts were interrupted when Jake came through the swinging door. "Our kitchen staff is too efficient and I ran out of things to slice and dice," he said. "Need some help?"

"Always." I stood on tiptoe and gave him a kiss.

The second keg was filled and Jake rolled it out of the way while I connected the next one. "Did you learn anything new at your breakfast this morning?" he asked.

"Maybe too much. I've been going over everything in my head, and nothing is connecting or making any sense."

"Like what?"

"Like everything." I sat down on the stairs that led up to the mash tun and told him what Paisley had said that morning. "I've been focusing too much on Candy's situation. I've assumed Felix killed Doodle because Felix was supposedly a bad guy. I learned from my dad to never make assumptions, but that's exactly what I've been doing. I lost sight of the facts."

Jake took care of the next keg. "It's only natural you'd think about Candy." He sat beside me on the step. "What else?"

I voiced what I'd been thinking about Felix seeing Candy for the first time and that I felt he only figured out who she was after the fact. Then there was Doodle's phone call and that he had to have called me for some other reason than fixing Candy up with Felix. And finally, that I didn't believe Felix was in Pittsburgh because of Candy. "The more I think about it, the more I'm convinced it's a coincidence. If he came here for Candy, he'd have done something by now."

"He could be biding his time. He has to know Candy told us about him. If something happened to her, he'd be the number one suspect."

"True." We both got up to do the next keg. "But I still don't think that's why he's here."

"That doesn't rule out Felix killing Doodle, though."

"No, it doesn't. Yesterday, Mitch said it might have just been a burglary attempt that went wrong. And considering Paisley saying how Rhonda's estranged husband died, I'm wondering if they're connected. A brother and a husband are both killed during break-ins? Seems a little fishy."

"When did the husband die?" Jake asked.

"Paisley didn't say, but Felix has been with the group for six months so it would have been before that."

"Six months is a long gap between the crimes."

"I know. But let's say Felix killed Roy Williams for whatever reason. He didn't find whatever it was he was looking for in Roy's apartment, so he gets a job with the band by telling Bruce he's a friend of Roy's. Felix thinks Doodle has what he's looking for and he gets wind that Doodle called me. He's worried that Doodle figured out his connection to Candy and is about to tell me, so he steps up his search for whatever it is he's looking for. He breaks in to Doodle's house and searches it. He doesn't find anything and the next day confronts Doodle in the rehearsal space. Doodle doesn't have any idea what Felix is talking about, but Felix has given himself away, so he kills Doodle and stuffs his head into his sousaphone."

Jake laughed. "I can't believe I actually followed all that. And it sort of made sense."

I punched his arm.

"Ow!"

"That didn't hurt, you big baby." I connected another keg to fill.

"If your theory is true," Jake said, "what is Felix after?"

"That's what we need to figure out. And I think I might know where to start."

CHAPTER SEVENTEEN

"So, what's your plan, Sherlock?" Jake asked.

"I don't have one," I said. "Not exactly anyway."

"What do you have then?"

"Paisley mentioned that she'd like to show me some of her brother's paintings at Rhonda's house. It's probably the only way I'll get to talk to Rhonda. I can't imagine her giving me the time of day otherwise. If that doesn't work, I'll talk to Bruce. I can make up some reason I need to talk to him about this coming weekend."

"That's all well and good, but what do you hope to accomplish by talking to them? If Felix is searching for something, they're not going to know about it."

Jake moved the filled keg out of the way, and I connected

the next one. "Maybe not," I said, "but they might inadvertently say something that gives me some kind of clue."

"I think that's a stretch," he said.

"It's all I've got right now." We discussed it more while we finished kegging. I was convinced this was the best option at the moment. Jake wasn't so sure, but he offered to go with me if I made arrangements with Paisley to go to Rhonda's.

After Jake rolled the last filled barrel into place, he returned to the kitchen and I got started on a brewer's least favorite job—cleaning up.

Two hours later, I grabbed a sandwich for my dinner and took it back to my office. After I ate, I found Paisley's number in my phone and called her. As I expected, she was thrilled to hear from me. It was a full five minutes before I could get a word in. She rambled on about how much she had enjoyed breakfast, and Candy was so nice, and we should do it again soon. I felt sorry for her. She wanted a friend so badly. She was a nice person, but I was sure her constant chattering drove any potential friends away.

When she finally took a breath, I said, "I'd like to take you up on your offer to see some of your brother's paintings."

"Oh, wonderful! You will love them so much. I can take you to Rhonda's now if you'd like."

I was hoping that's what she would say. Nicole had come in at four and she was closing tonight so it wouldn't be a big deal if I left for an hour or two. "Are you sure it's no trouble? I don't want to interrupt your dinner."

Paisley assured me that she had eaten already and Rhonda usually skipped dinner or ate very late. She offered to pick me up, but I convinced her to give me directions instead and I'd meet her there. The house was in Mount Lebanon—an area I wasn't very familiar with, but that's what GPS was for. When I hung up, I headed to the kitchen to see if Jake could break away and come along.

Fifteen minutes later we were on our way. Jake offered to drive after I told him where Rhonda's house was. He was somewhat familiar with Mount Lebanon. When he'd played hockey in high school, some of the games were held at an ice rink there. Forty minutes later, we turned onto the correct street.

The farther we drove up the street, the larger the houses got. Rhonda's house was the last one at the end of a cul-de-sac. "Wow," I said. "I had no idea." Although from the way Rhonda dressed and the car she drove, I probably should have figured her house would be the largest on the block.

Jake steered into the driveway between two stone pillars. The driveway opened up into a large parking area in front of a three-car garage. We pulled up beside an old Volkswagen Beetle. Paisley opened the door and got out. I wasn't surprised that was her car.

"Welcome to the old homestead," she said when we joined her.

"Homestead?" I said.

"Yep. I actually grew up in this house, believe it or not.

It's Rhonda's now. For some unknown reason, my parents put it in her name before they died. Not that I mind. If Rhonda sells it, it still has to be split three ways—" She shook her head. "I guess it's two ways now. That's going to take some getting used to. Walter and I lived here for a while after Mom and Dad died, but I bought my own place three years ago. I got tired of Rhonda telling me what to do all the time. Walter got tired of it and moved out, too."

We followed her to the front door while she talked. She reached into her handbag and pulled out a key ring that had to have at least a dozen keys on it. "I can come and go as I please," Paisley said as she unlocked the door. "Sometimes I expect Rhonda to change the locks because I've interrupted one too many dinner parties, but so far she hasn't. Here we are."

The door opened into a two-story-tall foyer with a marble tile floor. The walls were painted an inviting cream color. A cherry hall table stood against one wall, and two wing chairs covered in a bright floral print were situated on the opposite side of the foyer. There was a curving staircase straight ahead that was carpeted in a warm, deep beige color.

"This is beautiful," I said.

"Rhonda did all this," Paisley said. "Actually, she paid someone to do it. She didn't do the work herself. But she did design it and pick everything out."

"She has good taste," Jake said.

Paisley shrugged. "I guess so. It's a little too stuffy for me."

I tried to imagine what her house looked like. I envisioned an eclectic mishmash of whatever struck her fancy at the moment.

Paisley called her sister's name, and a few seconds later Rhonda appeared at the top of the stairs. "I told you—" Rhonda stopped when she saw us. "What's going on?" She didn't sound happy.

"I brought them to see some of Walter's paintings," Paisley said.

"Now? This is not a good time." Rhonda started down the stairs.

Paisley made a sound of dismissal. "It never is for you. We'll stay out of your way."

Rhonda reached the bottom of the steps. "I'm expecting guests in an hour. I told you that earlier."

The last thing I wanted to do was watch the sisters spar. "Maybe we should do this another time, Paisley," I said.

Paisley ignored my suggestion. "We're here now," she said. "It won't take long."

Rhonda grabbed Paisley's arm. "I said no. Not now." She turned to Jake and me. "This really is a bad time."

"We understand," Jake said.

"I'm sorry if this caused problems for you," I said to Rhonda.

"I'm used to it," she said. "If you really want to see Walter's paintings, why don't you stop in tomorrow sometime? I'll be here until noon."

"They want to see them now," Paisley said. She sounded like a whiny teenager.

I was beginning to be as annoyed with Paisley as her sister was. "Tomorrow morning would be great," I said. "Around ten?"

Rhonda said that would be fine. Jake and I said good-bye

and hurried out of the house, leaving Paisley pouting beside her sister.

Back in the truck, Jake said, "That was a little weird."

"And uncomfortable. If I'd have known Paisley was going to pull something like that, I'd have contacted Rhonda myself. I'm surprised Rhonda even offered to show us the paintings. I expected her to throw us out and tell us to never come back."

He put the truck in gear. "She probably felt bad because her flaky sister dragged us all the way out here."

"Probably." I hoped Paisley didn't make an appearance tomorrow morning. Contrary to what I'd thought up until then, it would be easier to talk to Rhonda without her sister being there.

The next morning after I did my usual brewery duties, I headed back to Rhonda's house—solo this time because Jake had to wait for a delivery. When I arrived, I was thankful that Paisley's VW wasn't in the driveway. Rhonda must have been waiting for me—she opened the door before I even rang the bell.

"Come in," she said. She was as impeccably dressed as she'd been every time I'd seen her. Today she wore charcoal slacks and a royal blue blouse. "Would you like some coffee?"

I said I would and followed her through the foyer and down a hallway to the rear of the house. Her kitchen was exactly what I expected. High-end appliances, granite counters, and white cabinets. She motioned for me to have a seat at the large island in the center of the room. She poured coffee into two mugs and brought them over with a small pitcher of cream and a bowl of sugar.

She sat down beside me. "First, I want to apologize for the way I treated you at Walter's funeral. I was angry at Walter for dying and at Paisley for . . . being Paisley. And I'm sorry about the fiasco last night. My sister can be challenging at times."

"I'm sorry I intruded," I said.

"Paisley intruded. You didn't know any better." Rhonda poured a minute amount of cream into her coffee and stirred it. "Enough about my sister. Why did you want to see Walter's paintings? It's not like you knew him well. From what Bruce said, you only met them recently and hired them to play at your pub."

I'd thought long and hard about what to tell her if she asked why I wanted to see the paintings. I considered making up a story about wanting to buy one, but I was a terrible liar. Besides, what if the paintings weren't anything like what were represented on Doodle's website and were horrible? The paintings weren't the reason I wanted to talk to her anyway. I really wanted to know why Doodle had called me and if it had anything to do with Felix. I'd stick as close as possible to the truth without mentioning Felix.

"Your brother called me a couple of days before he died and said he had something to tell me. Ever since then, I've been trying to figure out what it was. When I found out he was an artist, I wondered if it had something to do with that somehow."

"He didn't tell you why he wanted to see you?"

"Not really."

Rhonda sipped her coffee. "But he gave you a hint."

I had hoped Bruce had mentioned some of this to her. It made me wonder why he hadn't. He knew Doodle had called me. "Nothing that made any sense. He said it was important, though."

She put her cup down. "Don't you think it was rather odd that someone who was practically a stranger called you out of the blue like that?"

"A little," I said. "That's probably why it bothers me so much."

Rhonda pushed her cup aside. "Walter wasn't flighty like Paisley. He wouldn't call and not give you some idea of what he wanted."

She wasn't going to give up. I could be as stubborn as she was. "I really wish he had." I shrugged. "I guess we'll never know."

She looked like she was going to press further, then changed her mind. She pushed herself out of her seat. "If you still want to see Walter's paintings, come with me."

I followed Rhonda back through the foyer, up the stairs, and down a hallway. She opened the last door on the left, which opened up into a large room with windows on two sides. "My brother liked to paint in here because of all the natural light. Until he bought his own house, that is. He moved everything out—all his canvases, paints, easels, you name it—and most of his paintings. He only left a half-dozen here. Bruce has sold three of them so far." She sighed. "I guess eventually I'll have to go to Walter's house and pick everything up."

"How many paintings did your brother take with him?"

"Probably twenty or thirty. I don't remember exactly how many."

If Doodle had taken that many paintings to his house, where were they? Surely he hadn't sold them all. They weren't in the room with the few art supplies I'd seen. I hadn't gone upstairs, though. Maybe they were on the second floor.

Rhonda opened a closet door on the other side of the room and pulled out two sixteen-by-twenty-inch canvases and leaned them against the wall.

I picked up the first one to get a closer look. It must have been one I'd seen on Doodle's website because it seemed vaguely familiar. I didn't know a lot about art, but I knew this was done in the impressionist style. It was a landscape of rolling hills covered in purple flowers. "This is beautiful," I said. "Your brother was very talented."

"Yes, he was," Rhonda said. "I'm thinking about keeping that one and having it framed. Walter wasn't happy with it, though."

"I don't see anything wrong with it."

"He was very particular. Every detail had to be perfect."

"Just curious, but was he the same way with music?"

"He was," she said. "He could play almost any instrument from the piano to his ridiculous sousaphone." She shook her head. "I told the police I never want to see that awful thing again. I hope they destroy it."

I didn't know what to say to that so I put the painting down and picked up the other one. This one was done in some kind of modern style. It also looked familiar. And ugly.

"Bruce thinks he can get a buyer for that one," Rhonda said.

"I know someone who owns an art gallery if you need help with that." I told her about Philip Rittenhouse.

"I've heard that name before," she said. "I'll keep it in mind. Thank you." She took the painting from me and returned the two pieces to the closet. She opened an adjacent door and pulled out a much larger canvas—probably measuring about two feet by four feet. It was covered with a white sheet. "Walter was very proud of this one." She leaned it against a wall and removed the sheet.

I could see why he'd been proud of it. It was an excellent reproduction of Da Vinci's famous *Last Supper*. When I lived in Germany, I'd taken a trip to Italy and had seen the original, which was huge, and painted directly on a convent wall. I remembered reading somewhere that it was the most reproduced painting in the world. I asked if her brother had been to see the original.

She nodded. "He'd been to Europe many times over the last ten or fifteen years. He'd always return with new ideas. My deceased husband went with him on the last trip."

"Paisley mentioned you'd been married."

Rhonda covered the painting again and slid it into the closet. "I'm sure she told you all the sordid details as well— most of them fictitious. Despite what she thinks, I loved my husband."

"She didn't say much, just that you'd had a big fight and he moved out."

"She loves to tell that story. And I'm sure she told you he was murdered when it was a simple fall down the steps.

Our so-called big fight was a minor spat, and the separation was only temporary. He would have moved back in."

I wasn't sure which of them to believe. Why would he move out if everything was hunky-dory?

We went back downstairs, and I thanked her and went on my way. I was glad to have seen the paintings, but they didn't get me any closer to figuring anything out. I still had no way to prove what Felix was up to. And I was beginning to think I never would.

CHAPTER EIGHTEEN

𝕴 got back to the brew house in time for the lunch hour. We had a steady crowd but it wasn't terribly busy. Later that afternoon after I'd filled Jake in on my morning adventure, he was bent over helping me change out a keg when I heard the door open. I glanced up. "Crap."

"What?" Jake said, straightening up.

Victoria sashayed into the pub.

"I thought she went back to New York," I said.

"So did I."

She spotted us and came over to the bar. "Hello, you two," she said. "My, what a glamorous job you have."

From her tone of voice I knew she didn't mean that in a positive way, but I went along with it. "It's the best job in the world."

"I'm sure it's just perfect for you."

In other words, I was the lowest of the low and not fit to shine her imaginary tiara.

All the seats at the bar were occupied, but one man noticed Victoria standing there and he jumped up and offered her a seat. She gave him a smile like he was the only man in the world. "Thank you so much," she gushed. "You are so sweet." She slid onto the empty stool. He asked if he could buy her a beer. She gave him another smile and told him she only drank champagne, "which they aren't classy enough to serve here." He didn't quite know what to make of that, but I'd bet he was sorry he gave up his seat. He moved to the other end of the bar.

Jake leaned on the bar. "What are you doing here, Victoria? I thought you went home."

"I know that would make you very happy," she said. "I decided to stay another week and take my painting home with me. I don't want to take any chances with it."

"Philip would make sure you got it," I said.

"That's not the point. I paid a lot of money for that painting and I want to enjoy it. Besides, the Carnegie Museum of Art is bringing some dignitaries of some sort to see it on Thursday night. I thought it would be beneficial to me to be there. Come to think of it, Jake, you should come. Maybe one of them has a connection to a more prestigious restaurant. You don't want to work in a beer joint the rest of your life."

Beer joint? My hands curled into fists. I began counting to ten but only made it to two before Jake spoke up.

"You still don't get it, do you?" His voice was dangerously low. "This is exactly where I want to be. You can take your prestigious events and upscale gala of the week and shove them right up your fancy—"

"Now, now, old chap." Tommy's voice drowned out Jake's last word. I hadn't seen him come in. He stood behind Victoria and she spun around on her seat.

"And who are you?" she snapped.

He made a short bow. "Tommy Fleming. Former agent of the Queen herself. And who might you be?" He was going full throttle British on her.

She put a hand out like she expected Tommy to kiss it. He obliged and Victoria introduced herself.

"I should have known," he said. "My lovely wife, Candace, told me all about you."

"Candace? I don't believe I know anyone by that name."

I wasn't about to tell her. Let her try and figure it out.

"Anyway," Tommy said. "I've been very much looking forward to meeting you." He took her by the elbow and helped her down from her seat. "I'm considering some kind of investment, and I would love to hear all about that painting of yours." As he led her away, he turned to us and winked.

"I wonder what the old chap is up to," Jake said.

"Old chap? You sound just like Tommy." I watched as they sat down at a table by the window. "Whatever he's up to, it's got Miss Prissy Pants off your case."

Jake laughed. "Miss Prissy Pants?"

I nodded. "It was the best I could come up with without having to go to confession."

He pulled me close and kissed me on the forehead. "That's one more thing I like about you, O'Hara."

"What? Saving myself from having to say three Our Fathers and three Hail Marys?"

"Nope. Making me laugh and saving me from choking someone."

Nicole came in at four, and when the dinner hour turned out to be a little slow, I decided to head next door to Cupcakes N'at. Jake had left ten minutes earlier—he and Mike had gone to tonight's hockey game. The Penguins were playing the Rangers—Jake's former team. He was looking forward to seeing some of his old teammates, but he'd assured my brother he'd be rooting for the Pens.

Candy was cleaning the inside of an empty bakery case. She straightened up. "Can you believe we sold out of almost everything today? I don't think that's ever happened before."

"That's good, isn't it?" I asked.

"Good for the bank balance," she said, "but not so good when I think about coming in at three in the morning and doing all that baking. Thank goodness Mary Louise is coming in to help."

"Do you want to take a break? I'll buy the coffee."

She didn't even stop to think about it. She whipped off her apron and quickly washed her hands. In minutes, she had locked up and we jaywalked across the street to Jump, Jive & Java. When we got inside, I was disappointed to see that Kristie wasn't there. The part-time girl at the counter said she'd left an hour before. I ordered an iced mocha, and Candy wanted a pumpkin chai. We took our drinks to our usual table.

"Tommy said he stopped in to the pub earlier," Candy said.

I spooned some whipped cream from the top of my mocha. "Yeah. He took Victoria off our hands. He started talking to her about that painting."

"He thought if he could find out more about it, it might help him figure out if Josef was at the gallery for a reason other than he's an art aficionado." She took a drink of her chai. "How is the security at that gallery?"

"Fine, I guess. I really don't know. I can't imagine that it wouldn't be state of the art, especially with the Vermeer. Are you thinking Felix is planning on stealing it?"

"I'm not sure," she said. "It doesn't seem like something he would do, but it's been many years since I knew him. Victoria invited us—well, Tommy anyway—to the gallery on Thursday night."

"She invited Jake, too. I'm not sure if it was extended to me, though. He pretty much told her where she could stuff the invitation."

Candy laughed. "Tommy told me about that. We're planning to go—and you should, too. Josef may decide to show up if he's really interested in that painting."

"I'll try to convince Jake, although personally, I'd be ecstatic not to have to see her again. And speaking of paintings," I said, "I saw some of Doodle's." I told her about what happened the previous night and that morning, then asked if she remembered seeing any paintings in Doodle's house.

"I didn't see any at all—even upstairs. I may have missed a closet or two, but if he had twenty to thirty paintings, surely there would have been some evidence of them."

"I guess it's possible he sold them."

Candy was skeptical. "That many? I doubt it." She finished her chai. "We need to get back in that house."

"How do you propose we do that? We can't exactly break in."

"Why not?"

"The first reason would be that it's illegal. That about does it for me."

She tapped her fingernails on the table. "Maybe we could ask Paisley to let us in. We don't have to tell her why. We can say we know someone who might want to buy the house. Something like that."

"I suppose." I wasn't thrilled with the thought of being with Paisley again—or even talking to her for that matter. I'd rather deal with Rhonda, but unless she was willing to meet us at Doodle's, I'd have to make the trek to Mount Lebanon again. Then again, maybe Paisley would just give us a key and we could let ourselves in. "I'll give Paisley a call first thing in the morning."

"How about now? I'm done for the day. Your pub is in good hands. We could check out the house and be back here in a couple of hours."

She had a point so I made the call. Paisley answered on the first ring and said she was on her way out, but had to go past the house. She'd unlock it and we could lock it back up when we left. I went back to the pub and told Nicole where I'd be and to call me if there were any problems.

Doodle's house hadn't been vacant very long but it already had that musty, closed-up odor to it. Paisley had left the door unlocked as promised. The living room was mostly as I remembered it, other than the fact that the spot where the TV had been was now vacant. Since Rhonda hadn't been here since Doodle's death, Paisley must have taken it—or maybe she'd given it to one of the other band members.

I followed Candy into the next room, which in most of these types of homes was the dining room. The papers and sheet music were still strewn all over the floor. Some empty canvases, brushes, and tubes of paint were still there as well. I tried to remember what else had been in the room, but nothing came to mind. There were no finished paintings anywhere. The kitchen was in the same condition.

"Should we try upstairs?" I asked.

"Might as well."

I led the way up the stairs. The second floor was an odd configuration that was common in some older homes—one where you had to go through the first bedroom to get to the second. I took a peek into the third room, which was separate from the other two. It was a bathroom. And not a neat one by any means. The pink 1950s-style tub looked like it hadn't been cleaned in this century. The rest of the room wasn't any better. I backed out quickly before I inhaled any of the mold spores.

Candy was already through the first bedroom and into the second. The first bedroom contained an unmade bed and not much else. I opened the closet, where all I found were some clothes and shoes. I joined Candy in the next room. This one had a large bay window and a lot of natural light. There were two empty easels, a couple of empty canvases, and a half-started painting leaning against a wall. There was a light sketch of a few figures on the canvas, but I couldn't make out exactly what they were. It almost looked like a biblical scene. An assortment of musical instruments—a guitar, a trumpet, a clarinet, and a trombone cluttered one corner of the room. I remembered Rhonda saying he was proficient on many instruments.

I opened the door to a small closet. It held towels, bed linens, and a few cleaning items that apparently Doodle hadn't known how to use. There were some paint supplies including some brushes that were marked *Badger Hair*, and a container of varnish.

But there were no paintings in sight. "I wonder where they are," I said.

"He probably sold them or gave them away," Candy said as we went back downstairs. "Why are you so gung-ho to find them anyway?"

"The truth is, I don't know. The paintings might not have anything at all to do with Doodle's murder. It just seems like there's a piece of a puzzle missing. I know the police think his murder was the result of a break-in, but I still have a feeling it has something to do with Felix. I've been thinking a lot about why Doodle called and wanted to see me. I believe he found out whatever it is that Felix is up to and wanted me to warn you."

Candy smiled. "Maybe you should go to work with your dad. You're turning into quite a detective."

"Far from it," I said. "I just like things to make sense, and nothing about any of this makes any sense at all."

"We'll figure it out."

The one place neither one of us had checked yet was the

basement, so at my suggestion, we headed to the kitchen. The door to the basement creaked on its hinges when I opened it. I found the light switch on the wall easily, flicked it on, and the stairs and basement were flooded with light. Candy followed me down the old wooden staircase. Doodle's cellar was surprisingly neat and clean—much more so than the rest of his house. The cement floor was a little bit dusty, but the cinder block walls were clean and painted a bright white. There was a folding banquet table near one wall with pieces of some type of cloth on top. On the floor beside the table were strips of wood. "What do you make of these?" I asked Candy.

She touched the cloth. "Between this and the wood, it looks like maybe he was making his own canvases."

That made sense. "Maybe it's cheaper than buying the manufactured ones. Seems like a lot more work to me."

Several gray metal shelving units lined an adjacent wall. One unit was filled with canned goods and another held labeled plastic containers. I moved closer to read the labels. *Lead white. Red ochre. Vermilion. Ultramarine.* I picked up a container and shook it. It was a powder. "Are these paints?" I asked. "I thought they came in tubes."

Candy checked out one of the containers. "I guess he used homemade paints to go on his homemade canvases." She pointed to another container on the shelf marked *Linseed oil.* "Maybe he mixed them with that."

"Don't you think that's a little weird?"

She shrugged. "Maybe. You should ask your gallery owner friend."

That was a good idea. The other shelves contained a

couple of heat lamps and a container of varnish similar to what I'd seen upstairs. Once again, there were no finished paintings anywhere.

As we reached the top of the stairs, I heard the front door open. "Paisley must have come back." I was about to call to her when I heard a man's voice.

"Who's there? Whoever you are, you'd better come out now. And for the record, I have a gun."

CHAPTER NINETEEN

Candy shoved me behind her.

"I'm saying it one more time," he said. "Who's there?"

It had taken me a few seconds, but I recognized the voice. "Bruce?" I came out from behind Candy. "It's me. Max O'Hara." I moved to the dining room with Candy right behind me.

"Max?" Bruce Hoffman stood at the other end. He wasn't carrying a gun. "What are you doing here?"

"Paisley let me in." I told him the same tale we'd given Paisley—that we knew someone who was interested in buying the house.

"Leave it to Paisley to scare both of us half to death." He

gave us a half smile. "Sorry about the gun thing. I thought you might be burglars."

Candy glared at him. "Do we look like burglars? You're lucky we aren't. If you ran into a real intruder who was armed, you'd be dead by now."

I put a hand on her arm. "It's okay. He'll know better for next time."

She gave him one last glare, then said she'd be on the front porch.

"What's up with her?" Bruce asked.

"She's just a little sensitive on the subject of guns." I couldn't very well tell him it probably reminded her a little of the encounter with Felix in Prague all those years ago. "What brings you here?"

"I stopped to pick up a few more things. Rhonda doesn't need or want any of the household goods, so I'm getting rid of them for her. I gave Manny the TV, and a buddy of his is going to take the sofa."

"It's nice of you to help them out."

He shrugged. "Rhonda said you'd been to see her."

I told him about the visit and that I'd seen a couple of Doodle's paintings.

"Doodle was pretty good with the brush."

"He was," I said. "Rhonda told me he took most of his paintings with him when he moved out but I didn't see any here."

"I took them for safekeeping. Empty house and all that. I didn't want someone coming in and stealing them."

"Makes sense to me."

There was a pause, then Bruce said, "Well, if you're done here, I can lock up."

I took the hint and started for the door.

"By the way," Bruce said, "did you ever figure out why Doodle called you?"

I shook my head. "Unfortunately, no."

I still thought it had something to do with Felix and Candy and what had happened in the past, but I didn't want Bruce to know that. The first thing he'd do would be to tell Felix.

Candy opened the door. "Are you ready to go yet?"

"I'm coming." I was glad she'd interrupted. I told Bruce good-bye, and within minutes Candy and I were on our way back to Lawrenceville.

It was eight by the time I got back to the pub. I had dropped Candy off at her house first, declining her invitation to come in. The pub wasn't especially busy, and when I told Nicole she could leave early, she took me up on it. I'd been working about an hour when Marcus Crawford came in. I grabbed a couple of menus and greeted him. "Is Philip joining you?" I asked.

"Nope. I'm all by my lonesome tonight."

I led him to a small corner table. "How's this?"

"Perfect."

"How is the store coming along? Do you have an opening date yet?"

Marcus smiled. "It's going great. I'm shooting for a soft

opening the last week of this month then the grand opening will be the first of October."

"That's great. I think your place will be very popular. We needed something like that in the neighborhood."

He gave me his drink order, and I left him to peruse the menu. When I returned with the stout he'd ordered, he asked me to join him. I went back to the bar and pulled a stout for myself and returned to the table. He gave his meal order to Cassie, who asked if I wanted anything. I started to tell her no, then realized I was hungry so I ordered my favorite appetizer—Buffalo chicken pierogies.

"That sounds like a winner." Marcus grinned. "Not exactly a health food, though."

"Don't worry, I'll share."

"I love this neighborhood," he said. "Everyone is so nice. Candy keeps trying to feed me. Daisy brought me a plant yesterday. Ken at the deli wants to stock some of my tea. Ralph up at the hardware store is giving me a huge discount. And Kristie has the best coffee anywhere." He grinned. "Before you ask, I consider coffee a health food." He held up his glass. "And so is this. They're both full of antioxidants."

I laughed. "Good to know."

He asked if I planned on coming to the gallery on Thursday evening.

"I'm not sure."

"I don't blame you. I don't think I'd be going if it wasn't for Philip."

I asked him why although I was pretty sure I knew the reason.

"Let's just say I'm not exactly fond of that client and leave it at that." Marcus sipped his beer. "So, why don't you know if you're coming to the gallery on Thursday?"

"It's a long story."

"Let me guess." He sat up straight in his chair. He raised his hand like he was flipping imaginary hair over his shoulder. In a falsetto voice he said, "I was engaged to Jake when he was a famous hockey player, you know. I keep trying to get him a job in a real restaurant in a real city where he can be famous again. That Max person is a bad influence on him."

I barely heard the last part because I was laughing so hard. "She actually said that?"

Marcus was laughing, too. "Not in those exact words, but yeah. She likes to rub it in that Jake played professional hockey while I only played college football."

"That's terrible."

"She's nice as anything to Philip. It bugs me that he thinks she's this sweet, wonderful woman."

"He's not the only person who fell for her act," I said. "She didn't show her true colors to Jake for a long time."

"She seems pretty good at showing her best side to only people who can help her. I'm not one of them, so I get to see what she's really like. I tried saying something to Philip, but he thinks I'm imagining it."

"You're not."

Cassie brought the Buffalo chicken pierogies and two plates to the table, and conversation halted for a bit while we ate.

"These are awesome," Marcus said. "And definitely not health food."

I wiped my fingers on a napkin. "Comfort food."

He picked up another pierogi and dipped it into the ranch dressing. "In that case, I may need to order a second platter."

When his meal arrived, I left Marcus to eat in peace and went back behind the bar. The rest of the evening was quiet. We were able to get a head start on the daily cleanup, which usually only began after we locked the doors for the night. It seemed like a long time since I'd stayed this late. My staff knew exactly what to do even when I wasn't there to supervise, but it felt good to participate for a change. By eleven p.m., we had almost all of the work done and everyone got out on time.

Once I got home, I fed and played with Hops. Jake called after he got home from the game. He said the game had been tied and finally ended in a shootout with the Pens scoring the winning goal. After the game he and Mike had gone to a local bar with a few of his former teammates. Jake had to put up with a lot of ribbing because he'd been wearing a Penguins T-shirt. It was all good-natured and I think it did Jake good to hang out with them.

After that, I filled him in on what he'd missed while he was at the game, ending with, "Bruce said he took the paintings because he was worried about someone breaking in and taking them."

"If someone broke in, I doubt they'd bother stealing paintings," Jake said. "I don't think a common burglar would know how to fence something like that. If anything, the burglar would vandalize them."

"True. In any case, they're not there. Not that it matters. Candy asked why I was so focused on seeing Doodle's paintings, and I didn't know what to tell her. I said I was just trying to make sense of things. I don't like unanswered questions."

"There's nothing wrong with that," Jake said.

"I know." I paused for a second. "Marcus stopped in tonight. He wanted to know if we were going to the gallery on Thursday."

"Did you tell him no?"

"I said I didn't think we were."

"Good."

"I'm not so sure that's the right decision," I said. "I've been thinking."

"Oh, no." I could hear the smile in his voice. "I warned you about that."

"Ha ha. Very funny. I seem to remember saying exactly the same thing to you. I changed my mind about Thursday night. I think we should go." Jake didn't say anything so I continued. "Felix was there the last time when the painting was revealed, and if he's that interested in the Vermeer, there's a good chance he'll show up again. It might be the only way to find out what he's up to. Candy and Tommy are going, and if Felix really is after Candy, which I'm not sure he is at this point because he hasn't tried anything, we'd be there to protect her."

"I'm impressed," Jake said.

"Really?"

"Yeah. You managed to say all that in one breath."

"You're lucky this is a phone call, Lambert. Seriously, what do you think?"

"I'll go on one condition," he said.

"And what's that?"

"A condition is—"

"Jake! Be serious for a second."

"Like I started to say, I'll go on one condition. Keep Victoria as far away from me as possible."

"Deal." I was sure that Candy would be more than happy to help with that. It might not even be an issue. Victoria would be preening for the cameras and hobnobbing with the museum folks—provided that they lived up to her high standards.

We talked a little more then said good night. Hops sat on the bathroom sink while I got washed up, then made herself comfortable on the bed and fell asleep. Within minutes, I did the same.

Hops's claws digging into my stomach woke me at three a.m. I groggily lifted her off me and put her on the bed beside me. She let out a loud meow that was nothing like any of her usual noises. I sat up. "What's wrong, kitty?" I scratched the top of her head.

She meowed again, hopped down to the floor, and went to the bedroom doorway. She turned and looked at me like she expected me to follow.

"If you lead me to your food dish, you're in big trouble."

I slid out of bed. I always kept the bedroom door partially open so Hops could come and go as she pleased and didn't have to wake me to use her litter box. I opened the door all the way and followed Hops into the living room.

And that's when I heard the noise. Someone was rattling the handle and fiddling with my front door.

CHAPTER TWENTY

Hops slunk to the door and hissed. Even though the dead-bolt was locked, I rushed back into the bedroom and dumped a pile of clothes off the old straight-backed chair in the bedroom. I carried the chair into the living room and jammed the back of it under the doorknob. Then I grabbed my phone and dialed 911. I was tempted to yell at whoever was outside my door that I'd called the police, but if I did, I'd scare them away. It would be better if he was still there when the police arrived.

The noise outside the door stopped. Hops alternated between pacing back and forth in front of the door and coming over to where I stood and butting her head against my leg. I thought I was handling the situation very calmly until a hard knock on the door just about made me jump out of my skin. My voice was shaky when I asked who was there.

"Police." He gave me his name and I recognized him as the officer who had responded to a call at the pub a few months ago.

I moved the chair, picked up Hops so she wouldn't escape, and unlocked the door.

"You might want to see this." The officer pointed to his side of the door.

I pulled the door open all the way. Whoever had been messing with the handle had left a note for me, written directly on the door with a bold black marker.

GIVE IT UP.

"Give what up?" I said aloud. "What's that supposed to mean?"

"You don't have any idea?"

I had plenty of ideas but none of them made any sense. There were footsteps on the metal stairs and the officer shooed me back into my apartment. I hoped it was the note-leaver coming back so he could be arrested—after he cleaned the ink from my door. I was slightly disappointed it wasn't, and more than slightly surprised that it was Vincent Falk.

"Is everything okay here?" he asked.

The officer looked a little confused. "Fine. Why are you here? I didn't request a detective."

"I was in the neighborhood and heard the call," Vince said.

I stepped back out into the hallway. "Vince and I are friends." It was probably news to Vince. To me as well.

The officer looked at Vince then at me and smiled. "Oh, I get it."

My face grew hot and I was sure it was beet red. "Not that kind of friend! We're acquaintances. Actually he almost arrested me once . . ." I didn't know what else to say.

Vince looked like he was trying not to smile. "I believe this is the first time I've ever seen you speechless, Max." He turned to the officer. "Her dad and I are partners. When I heard the call, I thought I should check and make sure she was all right."

After a bit of back slapping between the two, we finally went inside and I gave the officer my report. He photographed the note on the door, and Vince dusted the lock and the door for fingerprints. Unfortunately they were all smudged. Now I not only had black marker to clean off the door, I had black fingerprint dust as well.

The officer went on his way, but Vince didn't seem to be in a hurry to leave. It was almost my normal time to get up so I offered him coffee. He took a seat on the sofa. Hops decided he was trustworthy and curled up beside him. I handed him a mug and sat down.

"You were in the neighborhood?" I raised an eyebrow and gave him a slight smile. I knew where he must have been.

His cheeks got a little pink. It was kind of cute. "Yes, I was."

The romance between Vince and Kristie must be really heating up if he only left her place at three a.m. "Your secret's safe with me."

"It's not a secret. We're just keeping it low-key."

I laughed. "Low-key? With Kristie?"

"Good point," he said. "That's not why I'm here, though. What's going on that someone would put that message on your door? What does it mean?"

"I'm not sure what it means."

"Are you poking your nose in where it doesn't belong again?"

Two months ago that question would have made me angry. At the time Vince and I hadn't seen eye to eye on his case—the one in which he'd been sure that Jake and I had committed murder. When I had uncovered the real killer, he'd apologized and admitted he'd been wrong so I was willing to forgive and forget. "No. Not exactly anyway."

"Not exactly. I don't like the sound of that. Tell me it doesn't have anything to do with that body you found."

I couldn't do that so I didn't say anything.

"You can't stay out of trouble, can you?" He let out an exaggerated sigh. "I'm probably going to regret this, but tell me everything."

So I did. Most of it anyway. As far as Candy's story, I told him only that she had known Felix by another name when she was younger.

Vince finished his coffee and set his cup on the end table beside him. "Do you mind if I give you some advice?"

"I'd say I did mind, but I know you'd give it to me anyway."

"You've obviously shaken someone up enough to leave that note on your door. Take it seriously."

"That's it? That's your advice?"

He gave me a slight smile. "Don't worry, there's more. Tell Mitch Raines everything you've told me. Although it could be a coincidence that the woman's husband and brother died in apparent break-ins, he needs to know—if he doesn't already. He'll want to look into that." He stood. "I'd better get going."

I walked him to the door. "Thanks for checking on me."

He nodded. "Once you talk to Mitch, leave the investigating to him. Talk to your father, too—or I will."

"You'd tattle on me?"

"In a heartbeat," he said. He wasn't smiling—he was serious. "If something bad happens and Sean finds out I knew about this and didn't tell him . . ."

He didn't have to finish the sentence. "I get the picture. I'll make the calls."

"It was nice chatting with you, Miss O'Hara."

I smiled at the formality. I'd kind of missed it. "Likewise, Detective Falk."

After he left, I managed to clean the fingerprint dust off the door, but the marker was permanent. Three different cleaners did nothing. I even tried nail polish remover, but all it did was smear the letters. I didn't want to bother the rental company, so I'd get some paint and fix it myself. But first, I had to shower and get to work.

Ɉ was meeting Daisy at Beautiful Blooms at nine so I had just enough time to check all the fermenters before heading up the street. She had just unlocked the door to the shop when I arrived.

"Morning, Max," she said with a smile. "The center-pieces are all ready to go. I think you'll be pleased."

"I'm sure I will be if they're anything like the sample you made." Was that only two weeks ago? It seemed like it had been longer than that. It had been the same day I'd convinced her to go with us to the fire hall where Felix had recognized Candy. I couldn't believe my Oktoberfest week-end was only two days away.

I took a seat on a piano stool at the counter while Daisy went to the back room. She returned carrying two cardboard boxes and placed them on top of the counter. "Here they are," she said. "What do you think?"

I lifted one out of a box. It was even better than the pro-totype she'd shown me. Instead of a small dish holding creamy white mums and blue asters made of silk, she'd used a blue mason jar. In the center was a small beer stein orna-ment and a tiny blue and white checked Oktoberfest flag. To top it off, she'd tied thin blue and white satin ribbons around the rim of the mason jar. "This is perfect," I said. "I love it!"

"I wasn't sure about using the jars, but I like how they turned out," she said.

"The jars are just the right touch." I stood up. "I'll take this box then come back for the other."

"I have a better idea," Daisy said. "I'll carry the other box then we'll head over to Kristie's. I haven't had my morn-ing coffee yet. And you haven't filled me in on what's hap-pened since we were at Hartwood Acres."

"Deal."

We walked to the pub, put the boxes on top of the bar,

then I locked the door again and we headed across the street. Jump, Jive & Java was living up to its name. The place was definitely jumping. The line was almost to the door, but Kristie and another barista worked quickly to serve everyone, and before long, it was our turn. I ordered my usual mocha and Daisy asked for a caramel latte.

"I heard you had a visitor last night," Kristie said as she made my mocha.

Daisy looked at me.

"It's a long story," I told her, then to Kristie, "When you get a break, come sit with us and I'll tell you all about it." I wondered how many times I'd said, *It's a long story*, over the past several days. I was getting a little tired of it.

"What was that all about?" Daisy asked after we sat down.

I said I'd fill her in when Kristie was able to join us. Five minutes later she plopped down into the chair beside me.

"Whew," she said. "I can't believe how busy it was this morning. This is the first chance I've had to catch my breath." She nudged me with her elbow. "So spill. What happened?"

"What did Vince tell you?"

"That when he was leaving my place at three—"

Daisy put a hand up in the air. "Whoa. Stop right there. Who is Vince and why was he leaving your place at three?"

Kristie raised an eyebrow. "Why do you think?"

"Oh." Daisy grinned. "Who is this mystery man? How long have you been seeing him? Why didn't you tell me you were seeing someone?"

"That's a lot of questions," Kristie said.

"Vince is my dad's partner," I said to Daisy.

"Wait," Daisy said. "Isn't he the one you called Vinnie

the Viper? The one who thought you and Jake killed that food critic?

I smiled. "One and the same."

Daisy shook her head in disbelief and looked at Kristie. "And you're seeing him?"

Kristie laughed. "That about sums it up. I'll tell you the whole story later. She turned back to me. "What happened last night? And what have I missed this week?"

I told them about the note left on my door, then backtracked and filled them in on the past week. I told them about Felix, Paisley, Rhonda, the paintings, and everything else that came to mind. "I have to call my dad and Detective Raines today, but Vince seems to think it's too much of a coincidence that Rhonda's husband and brother died in similar fashions. And the more I think about it, I agree with him. And as far as I'm concerned, it has to have something to do with Felix."

"Does this mean Felix really isn't after Candy?" Daisy asked. "I thought that was what this whole thing was about. That Doodle was going to tell you about Felix and Candy."

"I don't know. It could be that none of this is connected, or that it all is." We talked for another ten minutes, but never came to any kind of a conclusion. The more I talked and the more ideas we tossed around, the more confused I became. I returned to the brew house with a million thoughts swirling through my head. And none of them made any sense.

𝕴'd had luck in the past writing down all my theories. Jake wasn't due in for another twenty minutes and I had some time before we opened for lunch, so after I moved the two boxes of centerpieces from the top of the bar to a corner in my office, I sat down at my desk with a tablet and a pen.

I started by writing down the names of all the suspects, giving each of them his or her own column. Felix was number one. What did I know about Felix? One, Candy had known him by the name *Josef Bartek* in Czechoslovakia in the late 1960s. Two, he'd drawn a gun on Candy and Tommy, and Candy had shot him. I kept going. He joined the Deutschmen after Rhonda's husband, Roy Williams, was killed. He'd recognized Candy. He was at the gallery for the unveiling of the Vermeer. He was a frequent visitor to Saint Anthony's Chapel to see the relics. I tapped my pen on the desk. That was all I came up with for Felix at the moment. I could always add more later.

I had listed the other band members in the next few columns. Bruce Hoffman. Leader of the band, or at least the contact person. Involved with Rhonda Dowdy Williams. Helped Doodle sell some of his paintings. Manny Levin was the other band member. I realized I knew nothing about him. He hadn't been on my radar at all. I made a note to find out more.

The next two columns belonged to Doodle's sisters. Rhonda's husband and brother had both died under unusual circumstances. According to Rhonda, Roy had died from a fall. Her sister thought he'd been murdered. Rhonda had been persistent in questioning me about why her brother had wanted to see me. She'd been very unfriendly toward me at the cemetery and again at Hartwood Acres. She'd been pleasant toward me at her house. Could that have been an act?

Then there was Paisley. She was clearly unstable. She was flighty and needy, and seemed to cause problems for her older sister. Had she also caused problems for Doodle? I remembered something she'd said at the cemetery—that her brother had promised to take care of her. What had she meant by that? Financially? Or emotionally?

As much as I hated to, I added another name to the list. Candy. I didn't honestly believe she'd killed Doodle, but with the history between her and Felix, I had to at least consider it. She had panicked when Felix recognized her. I had never seen her that upset. And I'd found her riffling through the drawers in Doodle's house. She'd been with Jake and me when we found Doodle, but that didn't mean she couldn't have been there earlier. I felt like a traitor even thinking such a thing. My friend would never kill someone in cold blood. Shooting Felix had been in self-defense. She hadn't had a choice, and that fact had devastated her for years. That's why she had behaved the way she did after Felix recognized her.

But what about Tommy? I liked him, but what did I really know about him other than he'd been Candy's husband? She'd never even hinted that she'd been married. And she hadn't said why they'd broken up. Tommy could have known Felix was here all along. Maybe Doodle got wind of it somehow. Doodle was about to reveal it to me, so Tommy killed him. I didn't buy that theory, either.

What a useless exercise. I dropped my pen onto the desk. "This is getting me nowhere."

"I'd be happy to go nowhere with you," Jake said. He came into the office and kissed me on top of my head.

I stood and wrapped my arms around his waist. "I'm so glad to see you."

"Now that's the kind of welcome I like."

"Me, too." I rested my head on his chest. He smelled like Irish Spring soap, and the sound of his heartbeat made me want to stay there all day.

Jake noticed the scribbles on my tablet. "What are you working on?"

I sighed. "A suspect list. And so far, a complete waste of time."

"Mind if I take a look?"

"Be my guest." I reluctantly let go of him and took a step back.

He quickly read what I had written. "I wouldn't call it a waste of time. It's a good list."

"But it doesn't narrow it down. Anyone on there could have killed Doodle. There are way too many unanswered questions, especially after what happened this morning."

Jake put the tablet back and half sat on the corner of the desk. "What happened this morning?"

I told him about the note left on my door.

"Why didn't you call me? I would have come right over."

"I know, but it wasn't necessary. I called the police, and a patrolman came and took my report. Even Vince stopped to check on me."

"Vince? Vince Falk? Why would he do that?"

Jake didn't know about Kristie and the detective. "I just found out the other day that Kristie and Vince have been seeing each other."

He looked as surprised as I had been. "Kristie and Vinnie the Viper. Interesting combination," he said. "I never would have figured they'd get together. They're complete opposites."

"Anyway, Vince was leaving Kristie's place around three this morning, heard the call, and decided to see if I was all right."

"I can't believe I'm saying this, but I'm glad he stopped to check on you," Jake said. "We kind of avoided each other for the most part at your parents' on Sunday, but he did seem . . . I don't know . . . different. Maybe even human."

I gave Jake a little smile. "Who knows? You could even be friends someday."

"I wouldn't go that far. We'll have to settle for tolerating each other." Jake picked up the tablet again, changing the subject. "You know what you're missing here?"

"Everything?"

"No, only one thing. If Doodle's murder and the note left on your door are related, we just need to figure out which one of these suspects thinks you're getting a little too close. Who on this list wants you to give up the search?"

CHAPTER TWENTY-ONE

Figuring that out was easier said than done. Any one of the people I'd listed could believe I was getting close to discovering who killed Doodle. And if he or she thought that, they knew a lot more than I did. I was about as far away from knowing who the killer was as I could get.

After the lunch rush, I retreated to my office again and called my dad. I was happy Vince hadn't squealed on me yet.

"Are you all right?" Dad asked when I'd finished telling him what had happened.

"I'm fine. It was a little scary at first, but now I'm annoyed that I have to paint my door."

"Aren't you glad you listened to me and kept your dead-bolt locked?"

I laughed. "Yes, I am." His phone beeped that he had

another call coming in, so that was the end of our conversation.

I called Mitch Raines next and got his voice mail. I said I had some important information and requested that he call me back. I hoped he wouldn't take too long to do so. I had decided that as soon as I passed the information off to him, I was done with it. The only reason I'd gotten involved in this in the first place was because I'd been worried about Candy. Felix hadn't made a move on her, and at this point I didn't think he would. He was still up to something, but it wasn't up to me to figure it out. Unless something changed and he went after Candy, I was leaving the investigation up to the police.

Having made that decision, I felt like a weight had been lifted from my shoulders. I spent the rest of the afternoon preparing for our weekend celebration. When Nicole came in at four, I told her I had an errand to run and would be back shortly.

I walked up Butler Street to the Good Value Hardware Store located on a cross street not far from the brew house. The Galaxy Bar next door to the hardware store had a sign posted stating, *Under New Ownership*. I was sad thinking about the previous owner, Dominic Costello, who had been so worried I was going to steal his customers. Dominic had been murdered by the same person who had killed Kurt. Up until Dominic had been killed, I had believed he was behind Kurt's death and all the vandalism at the brew house. It had turned out someone else hadn't wanted the brewpub to open and committed murder to try and drive me out. I took another glance at the Galaxy and couldn't help thinking that Dominic would be glad to see the Galaxy live on.

The bell on the door of the hardware store tinkled as I entered. A few customers were browsing. I headed for the rear of the store, where Ralph Meehan had just hung up the phone. He smiled when he spotted me. Ralph and I had gotten off to a bit of a rocky start. He had been a good friend of Dominic Costello's and believed everything Dom had told him about me. I'd actually accused Ralph of murder at one point, but fortunately that was all in the past. We'd both learned our lessons.

"Max!" he said. "I haven't seen you for a while. How are you?"

"Busy as usual," I said. "You should stop in."

"I keep meaning to, but by the time I'm done here, I just want to get home."

"I know how that is. We're having an Oktoberfest party this weekend if that interests you."

"That sounds like fun," he said. "But I'm sure that's not why you're here. What can I get for you?"

I told him I needed a quart of white paint and explained why.

Ralph shook his head, making his gray comb-over flutter. "You sure get yourself into some situations." He went into the back room and returned with two cans of paint. "You'll need to use this primer first; otherwise the letters will bleed through."

I ended up leaving with primer, paint, a brush, a roller, and a paint pan.

The dinner hour was busy, and by seven I still hadn't gotten a return call from Mitch Raines. I left him another message, even though he might think I was nagging. Although I'd made the decision to let this go, I felt like I couldn't until I talked to the detective.

I'd just returned my cell phone to my pocket when Candy and Tommy entered the pub. I left Nicole to man the taps, greeted my friends, and led them to a corner table, where I plopped into a chair across from them.

"You look tired," Candy said.

"Gee, thanks," I said.

Tommy reached across the table and patted my hand. "You work too hard, my dear."

"It's not that. I was up at three a.m."

Before they had a chance to ask me why, Nicole brought two iced teas and a stout to the table and placed the stout in front of Tommy. "I brought the usual," she said.

"Iced tea isn't my usual drink," I said.

Nicole smiled. "I thought you could use the caffeine."

When she left, Candy said, "I told you that you looked tired. Why were you up at three?"

I told them about the note written on my door.

"Excellent!" Tommy grinned. "Most excellent."

"We must be getting close," Candy said. "We shook someone up."

I hadn't expected that kind of reaction. I thought they'd be concerned, especially since Candy was the mother hen type. "You're not worried?"

Candy gave me a look. "No. And you shouldn't be, either. It's a warning, that's all."

"And not a very good one," Tommy added.

"If this person wanted to harm you, he wouldn't have left

a note on your door," Candy said. "He'd have struck when you least expected it."

"If that was meant to be comforting, it's not working." I picked up my glass and took a sip. "It would have been nice if the person had told me exactly what I was supposed to give up. The investigation? Chocolate for Lent? Jake?" Jake. Could Victoria have left that note? It wasn't her style, but still . . .

"It wasn't Victoria," Candy said as if she could read my mind.

"How do you know that? She hates me and wants Jake back."

Candy rolled her eyes. "She probably doesn't even know what a permanent marker is, let alone how to use one. She wouldn't come down from her self-imposed pedestal to demean herself like that."

"She could have hired someone to do it," I said.

"Not likely," Candy said. "She wouldn't even know where to look. She doesn't exactly travel in the same circle with that type."

"It was Josef," Tommy said. "I'm sure of it. That's exactly his way. Until that last day in Prague, he always preferred the path of least resistance. He'd intimidate until the other person backed off."

"Have you gotten any information from your contacts?" I asked Tommy.

He shook his head. "I've been hitting a brick wall. Apparently there is no record of a Josef Bartek or a Felix Holt anywhere. No one is willing to tell me more than that.

Candace and I know very well that he existed—and still does. That makes me more suspicious than ever."

"Someone has to know something," I said.

"Oh, they know, all right," Candy said.

"Then why is it such a big secret? Why won't anyone tell you anything?" It didn't make sense to me.

"Three possible reasons, my dear." Tommy drained his glass. "One, Josef is still an active agent with whatever they're calling the KGB these days and the information is top secret. Two, he's defected and his record has been wiped for his safety."

"And number three?" I said.

Candy and Tommy exchanged glances before he answered. "He's gone rogue. Which makes him very dangerous. Very dangerous indeed."

Mitch Raines finally returned my call at ten that night. "Got your message," he said. "Sorry it took so long to get back to you. What's up?"

"There was a little incident at my apartment last night that I think is connected to Doodle's murder."

"How do you figure that?"

I told him everything that I'd told Vince early that morning, plus much of what I'd jotted down in the notebook on my desk. When I'd finished, the detective was quiet for so long that I thought the call had dropped. "Mitch? Are you still there?"

"I'm here. I'm just figuring out what to say."

What was there to figure out? "Just tell me you're going to look into all this."

"Max, I know you're trying to help and I appreciate that."

I knew what was coming next. I could tell by his tone of voice.

"But you're seeing something that's just not there. There is no evidence that Walter Dowdy's death was any more than a break-in gone wrong."

"What about his brother-in-law? Don't you find it suspicious that both of them died during a break-in?"

Mitch sighed. "Maybe a little, but it doesn't mean they're connected." He paused. "Look. If it makes you feel any better, I'll see if I can find the report from when Roy Williams died. If there's anything there, I'll look into it."

"What about the incident at my place this morning?"

"I just pulled up the report. The officer entered it as criminal mischief/vandalism."

"Vandalism?" I slapped my hand down on my desk. I felt tears forming in my eyes. When I got angry enough, I cried and I hated it. I took a deep breath and blinked. "It wasn't just vandalism. It was a threat. Someone wants me to back off, and it's got to be someone on that list I gave you. One of them killed Doodle. I'm sure of it."

I had been positive that Mitch would take what I told him seriously. It was a strange turn of events that Vince believed me and Mitch didn't. I'd have put my money on it being the other way around.

"I don't want to be the bad guy here," Mitch said. "Maybe it will turn out that you're right and I'm wrong. But as of now, there's no evidence that any of the people you mentioned committed murder. If I were you, I'd forget about it. If something changes, I'll let you know."

I sat at my desk for a long time after we disconnected. I felt so let down. I had hoped to turn the investigation over to the police like Vince had suggested. The weight that had lifted earlier now sat on my shoulders heavier than ever. It was up to me to figure out which of the people on my list had killed Doodle. And I was determined to do just that.

CHAPTER TWENTY-TWO

𝕴 woke at my usual time on Thursday morning—or maybe I should say Hops woke me at her usual time. I fed and played with her for a bit then headed to the brew house. Tomorrow night was the beginning of our Oktoberfest weekend, and I wanted to make sure all was in order. I had plenty of Oktoberfest beer, Jake had the food under control, and Nicole and my mom were coming in on Friday morning to help me and the rest of the staff decorate. I was happy to see we hadn't missed anything.

After making the rounds in the brewery and checking the gauges on the fermenters, I went next door to Cupcakes N'at. I needed to tell Candy about my conversation with Mitch last night and tell her about an idea I'd come up with on my way to work. Besides that, I was in dire need of a chocolate muffin. Candy and Mary Louise were both behind the counter waiting on the only two customers in the bakery.

We exchanged greetings, and since I hadn't seen Mary Louise for a few days, I asked her how she was.

She handed her customer the change from his purchase then gave me a smile. "Good as gold. What can I get for you?"

I pointed to the lone chocolate muffin in the case.

"These were very popular today," Mary Louise said.

Candy finished with her customer. "We're going to have to start baking more of them."

I paid for my purchase and asked Candy if she had a minute.

"Let's go for coffee." She turned to Mary Louise. "Can I get you anything?" She declined and Candy and I crossed the street to Jump, Jive & Java.

Kristie's part-time barista was working the counter, and Kristie was arranging a display of coffee beans in clear cellophane bags tied with colorful ribbons. "What do you think?" she said. "I'm trying something new. People keep asking if they can buy beans to take home and I finally took the hint."

"It's a great idea. I like it," I said.

"I do, too," Candy said. "I'll take two bags."

"Woo-hoo! My first sale." Kristie handed them to Candy. Once we'd ordered and paid, Kristie joined us at our usual table.

"Did the detective ever call you back?" Candy asked.

I nodded. "He wasn't impressed with what I'd told him. He's not going to do anything."

"You're not talking about Vincent, are you?" Kristie asked.

"Mitch Raines," I said.

Candy smiled. "We'd never talk about your cute little Vince unless we're talking about his cute little—"

"Candy!" Kristie and I said in unison.

"What? I was going to say dimple," she said. "Although come to think of it, he does have a cute little behind."

We all laughed.

"You're incorrigible," I said. "Can we get back on track here?"

"Spoilsport." Candy waved a hand in the air. "Go on."

"I was pretty upset last night when he told me he wasn't going to change his mind and I should just forget about the whole thing. I felt like he was telling me to be a good little girl and not to bother him anymore. I did some thinking after we hung up and I'm not going to forget about it. I'd hoped he would do the right thing then I could leave it up to him, but I can't do that. If he's not going to look for Doodle's murderer, then I am."

Candy squeezed my arm. "You mean *we are*. I'm as much involved in this as you are."

"I was hoping you'd say that." I leaned my forearms on the table. "I have a plan."

We spent the next fifteen minutes discussing the idea I'd come up with only that morning, then we split up to make some phone calls and put the plan into action.

The first person I'd called that morning had been Philip Rittenhouse, and when I explained what I wanted to do, he was willing to help us out. After that, I made the other calls and everything fell into place.

I watched the clock all day, willing time to move faster. Of course it didn't. As a matter of fact, it seemed to move slower. When five o'clock finally rolled around, Jake and I left the pub in Nicole's hands. I went home to feed Hops and change clothes. The gallery event tonight wasn't as formal as the opening and the unveiling of the Vermeer, so I chose a plain black shift dress and black low-heeled pumps. Grandma O'Hara's pearl necklace and earrings were a nice finishing touch.

Jake picked me up at six thirty so we'd be at the gallery by seven, before anyone else arrived. I nervously tapped my fingers on the armrest as Jake maneuvered through traffic on Baum Boulevard.

"Stop worrying," he said. "It's a good idea."

"But what if I'm wrong? I'm going to look like an idiot, and Doodle's murderer will still be out there somewhere."

He reached over and squeezed my knee. "I don't think you're wrong, but I am surprised Philip went along with it."

"I'm not. I explained to him that Doodle's paintings were very good. And he doesn't actually have to buy any of them. All he has to do is look at them."

By this time we'd arrived at the garage where we had parked the week before. Jake and I walked the short distance to the Gallery on Ellsworth. Philip greeted us at the door.

"Thanks for helping us out, Philip," I said. "I really appreciate it."

"You're welcome." He smiled. "I feel like I'm a character in an Agatha Christie novel. This will be fun."

I wasn't sure about the fun part. Nerve-wracking was more like it.

"I checked out the artist's website after you called me. I was impressed. Both his original works and his copies were very good. I tried to get into the Commissioned Works section, but it asked for a password. You don't happen to have it, do you?"

I'd forgotten all about that page on the website. I'd meant to ask Paisley about it. "No, I don't, but we can get it later."

"I have a few things to do," Philip said, "but make yourselves at home." He disappeared down a hallway, leaving Jake and me alone in the gallery.

"What did he mean by copies?" Jake asked.

"I don't know. I was wondering the same thing. Maybe he makes more than one of certain paintings." A wisp of a thought floated through my mind, but it was gone before I could grasp it.

Candy and Tommy arrived just then. Tommy looked dapper as usual in his black pinstripe suit and a blue tie that matched his eyes. He'd traded his umbrella for a shiny black lacquer cane with a brass knob on the top. Candy sparkled. Literally. Her outfit sported more sequins than a Rockette. She wore a black calf-length dress with a long gold-sequined jacket. Her shoes matched the jacket and so did the gold beret on her head.

"That's a lot of sparkle," I whispered to Jake as we went toward them.

"I know. I should have brought my sunglasses."

Tommy took my hand and kissed the back of it. "You look lovely, my dear."

"Thank you." I gave Candy a hug. "New outfit?"

She twirled around. "This should get Josef's attention, don't you think?"

It would get everyone's attention. "Definitely," I said.

A few other invited guests arrived. Marcus stopped to say hello, then went to talk to a friend who had just come in. So far there was no sign of Bruce, Manny, Rhonda, Paisley, or most importantly, Felix. When I'd called Bruce that morning and told him I knew a gallery owner interested in seeing Doodle's artwork, I told him to ask Manny and Felix to come, too. I made up a story that I wanted to talk to them all together about the party this weekend, and it would save time to do it tonight. He seemed to buy it, but now I wasn't so sure. What if they didn't show up? I didn't have an alternate plan.

They still hadn't arrived when Victoria made her grand entrance with two curators from the art museum. The way she fawned over them was downright nauseating. She hadn't acknowledged our presence at all even when Philip nodded his head in our direction. As far as she was concerned, it appeared we didn't exist. I was perfectly fine with that.

Philip had the Vermeer roped off to keep anyone who didn't know better from touching it, and he opened one end to give the museum people a closer look. One of them shook Philip's hand and I could tell he was congratulating him on his find. Victoria didn't seem to like that much and somehow directed the conversation back to her.

The crowd was much smaller than it had been at the opening last Friday—besides us, there were only a handful of people. Jake and I wandered around a bit, then went to stand with Candy and Tommy. We chatted for a few minutes then Jake nudged me. Felix Holt was coming through the door. When he spotted us, he went to the other side of the room, closer to the Vermeer.

Just as I was about to give up on the others, Bruce and Rhonda arrived, followed by Manny Levin. "Show time," I said. The plan was for me to greet and introduce them to Philip while Jake went to keep an eye on Felix. Candy and Tommy were posted by the door in case he tried to make a run for it. I pasted a smile on my face and greeted them.

"I'm glad you could make it," I said. "Philip is really excited to hear about the artwork."

"Thank you for arranging it," Rhonda said. She was elegantly dressed as usual in a black crepe pantsuit. Her gaze circled the room. "Walter would be very pleased."

"Felix arrived just before you did," I said. "Is Paisley on her way?"

Bruce shook his head. "She was having car trouble and said she couldn't make it."

"That's too bad." It might be a good thing. I wasn't sure Paisley was a good fit for this crowd.

"While you do your artsy thing, I'm gonna go find Felix," Manny said.

I didn't like the idea. I wanted Felix to move toward us so he could hear the conversation, but there wasn't anything I could do about it. I asked Bruce and Rhonda to follow me and I'd introduce them to the gallery owner. Philip saw us coming toward him and excused himself from the group standing in front of the Vermeer. Just as I had wanted, we were near enough to Felix that he would hear what was going on.

Philip shook hands with Bruce and Rhonda, and we exchanged small talk for a minute. I noticed Felix watching us closely while he mostly ignored Manny's attempts at engaging him in conversation.

Philip finally got down to business. "Rhonda, Max tells me you'd like to sell some of your late brother's paintings. I would love to take a look at them. I was impressed by the ones I saw on his website. When can I see them?"

Rhonda gave him a small smile. "I've enlisted Bruce to handle the sale of any paintings, if that's all right with you."

"Certainly," Philip said.

"I brought a few of the smaller ones with me," Bruce said. "I have them in the car."

"Perfect. If I like them, you can bring the others by in the morning and we'll talk business."

Victoria called to Philip, and he sighed. He handed Bruce a business card. "Bring in what you have, and take them back to my office." He pointed down a hallway. "I'll be back as soon as I can."

As soon as Philip was out of earshot, I went to part two of the plan to draw Felix out before Bruce disappeared and I didn't have a chance later. I said to Bruce, "Before I forget to tell you, I figured out why Doodle wanted to meet with me."

I watched Felix out of the corner of my eye, and if he was worried I knew anything, he didn't show it. His face showed no reaction at all.

But Bruce's did. A flash of surprise showed on his face before he said, "That's great. You can tell me all about it later." He turned to Rhonda. "I'm going out to get the paintings. I'll be right back."

Felix watched him the whole time, but didn't follow.

Rhonda and I made awkward conversation for what seemed like forever until Bruce returned carrying three bundles covered in brown paper. He moved past us and down the hall and Philip followed him back to the office.

Rhonda suddenly gasped. "Oh no." I turned in time to see Paisley shove one of the museum visitors away from the Vermeer. So much for having car trouble.

"I thought Paisley couldn't come," I said.

Rhonda didn't respond. Her face had paled as she stared at her sister.

Paisley stepped closer to the Vermeer then spun around to face the crowd. "Someone had better tell me what you're doing with my brother's painting."

CHAPTER TWENTY-THREE

Victoria stepped forward. "I don't know who you are, or who your brother is, but that painting belongs to me."

"No, it doesn't."

"Yes, it does."

They sounded like children arguing over a toy.

Rhonda rushed over to her sister and put an arm around her shoulders. "Paisley, honey. I think you're confused." Rhonda started to lead her away from the painting, but Paisley would have none of it.

Paisley shook off her sister's arm. "Don't patronize me. I'm not a child."

"Of course you're not," Rhonda said. She took Paisley's hand. "Why don't we go talk about this?"

So much for my plan. I had to do something. I hurried over to them. "Can I help?"

"Yes," Paisley said. "You can find out why my brother's painting is here."

Victoria put her hands on her hips. "For the last time, it's my painting. I own it."

"If you own it, then where's my money?" Paisley asked. "Walter promised to take care of me."

Something clicked in my brain. Philip mentioning copies. An anonymous seller. Homemade canvases. The powdered paints and linseed oil. Varnish. The locked page on the website. Doodle wasn't only an excellent artist, he was an art forger. But how was Felix involved? Were they in it together? Felix had contacts all over the world. It made sense.

But then another thought came to me. Maybe Felix wasn't involved at all. I'd been looking at the wrong person. Bruce was the one who handled the sales. He had removed the artwork from Doodle's house so no one could see it before he was able to unload it to unsuspecting buyers. Bruce probably sold just enough of Doodle's legitimate paintings to keep suspicion off them. What about Rhonda? Was she involved as well?

Victoria said, "I paid good money for that, and I'm taking it back to New York with me tomorrow." She glared at Rhonda. "If you're the sister of this lunatic, maybe you should look into getting her some help."

"I plan on doing just that," Rhonda said.

Paisley began crying. "I'm not crazy. Why doesn't anyone believe me?"

I hadn't noticed Candy coming over until she said, "I

believe you, dear." She put an arm around Paisley. "Remember me?"

Paisley looked up through her tears. "We had breakfast together. You were nice."

Rhonda and Candy exchanged a look, and Candy led Paisley away and sat her down in a chair on the other side of the room. I watched them for a moment—until Rhonda looped her arm through mine and I felt something hard press into my side.

"You know, don't you?" Rhonda said.

I glanced down at my waist. Rhonda's arm through mine was positioned so no one could see she had a gun. "Know what?" My voice sounded calm to my own ears. "I don't know what you're talking about."

"Don't be an idiot like my sister. I can see it on your face. As soon as Paisley mentioned money, the wheels started turning in your head. We're going to take a walk down that hallway and find Bruce."

My gaze swept the room. Victoria was ranting at Jake, and Tommy was with Candy and Paisley. I even looked for Felix—he was by the fake Vermeer talking to one of the museum curators. Manny was no longer with Felix. He must have gotten tired of being ignored and left. I didn't have any choice but to go with her. Hopefully, someone would notice I was gone before long.

When we reached the door to Philip's office, Rhonda shoved me into the room.

Philip's eyes opened wide when he saw the gun in Rhonda's hand.

"We have a problem, Bruce." Rhonda nodded her head toward me. "She knows."

"That is a problem." He reached under his jacket and drew his own weapon. "Both of you—over there." He pointed to the other side of the room.

Philip and I moved behind his desk and stood against the wall. His face was pale.

"There's more," Rhonda said. "Paisley is here."

Bruce swore. "And you left her out there? Are you nuts? This is just great." He swore again. "Once she sees it, she's going to tell everyone."

"She already did. No one believes her. They all think she's crazy."

"But for how long?" Bruce asked. "It's only a matter of time."

Philip had recovered from the shock a bit. "Would someone please tell me what's going on?"

Neither Bruce nor Rhonda answered him so I did. "Your Vermeer is a fake."

"Where did you get such a ridiculous idea?" Philip said. "It's been authenticated by several experts."

"Your experts were wrong," I said.

He shook his head. "It's not possible."

I wasn't going to convince him right now. I looked around the room searching for a way out of this mess. The office was large and I thought it must do double duty as a workroom. There was an oblong banquet-like table on the other side of the room where three unwrapped paintings lay. Bruce paced back and forth in front of the table.

"Wearing a track in the floor isn't going to help our situation," Rhonda said.

He stopped. "We need to get rid of these two and get out of here."

Philip's face whitened again. For some reason, I felt strangely calm considering one or both of them had killed Doodle—and possibly Rhonda's husband. Maybe it was the fact that there was still a roomful of people a short distance up the hallway, some of whom would be wondering where I was.

"That's not a good idea," I said.

"Shut up," Bruce said. "It's all your fault we're in this position."

"How is it my fault?"

"Because you wouldn't mind your own business," Bruce said. "You hired us to play at your party. That should have been the end of it. Instead you asked questions that were none of your business, you showed up at her brother's funeral, you showed up at our concert, you even showed up at Rhonda's house. I don't get it. Why do you care about any of it?"

"Maybe because someone died," I snapped. "Two people, as a matter of fact." I couldn't stop myself. "Which one of you killed Doodle? Or was it both of you?"

"My brother was in the wrong place at the wrong time. Neither one of us killed him," Rhonda said. "Right, Bruce?" He took a second too long to respond, and a look of horror crossed Rhonda's face. "You didn't." She leaned against the desk. "Tell me you didn't murder my brother."

Bruce stared at the wall. "I didn't have a choice. He was going to quit." He looked at me. "He found out your father was a cop. He said he was going to tell you everything so you could pass it on to him."

I'd never guessed that was the reason. I had been so wrong thinking it had been about Candy and Felix.

Suddenly, Rhonda pointed her gun at him and fired.

And that's when all hell broke loose.

The sound of screaming came from down the hall. Rhonda dropped the gun to the floor and fell to her knees. I nudged the gun out of her way with my foot. Philip stood frozen against the wall. The first person through the doorway was Felix, of all people. He glanced quickly at me and Philip, then went directly to Bruce.

Jake was right behind Felix, followed by Candy, Tommy, and Paisley. Jake gathered me into his arms and I clung to him. I'd been okay up till then but now I was shaking. Paisley knelt beside her sister and put her arm around her. Bruce must have still been alive because Felix had removed his jacket and was pressing it against his abdomen. I said a quick Hail Mary that he survived.

Police and paramedics arrived within minutes and everyone was ushered out of the room so they could work on Bruce. An officer helped Rhonda to her feet and had her sit in the chair at the desk. He took possession of both weapons.

Jake and I moved to the far end of the hall away from the gallery. "Are you all right?" he asked.

I nodded. "I'm okay."

"Hearing that gunshot and not knowing where you were scared me half to death," he said.

"Only half?" I gave him a little smile.

"Don't ever do that again, O'Hara."

"I didn't do it on purpose, you know."

"What the hell happened?" he asked. "Why were you back there? One second you were in the gallery and the next I didn't see you anywhere."

I told him.

"So Bruce killed Doodle," he said when I'd finished.

"Rhonda had no idea what he'd done."

"But she was still involved in the art fraud. What about Paisley?"

I shook my head. "I don't think she knew her brother was producing forgeries—at least as far as I could tell by her reaction to seeing the Vermeer. I mean the fake Vermeer. Speaking of which, where's Victoria?"

"I don't know. The last I saw her, she was talking to one of the museum people."

The paramedics brought Bruce out on a stretcher just then and we watched them wheel him down the hallway. He was still alive. I saw Candy and Tommy in the gallery as the stretcher rolled past and I suggested to Jake that we join them.

Candy enveloped me in a bear hug when we reached them. If she'd held me any tighter, I would have suffocated. I extricated myself as gently as possible. I didn't want to hurt her feelings. I smiled when she said the same thing Jake had, "Don't ever do that again."

I had to repeat my story and I imagined I'd be doing that for some time.

Felix had just come down the hall and entered the gallery as I finished, and when he saw us, he abruptly turned right.

He took two steps and stopped. A few seconds later, he turned around and headed toward us. Candy clutched Tommy's arm as if waiting for the worst. Instead of the confrontation I'd expected, Felix smiled. "Hello, Catherine." He nodded to Tommy. "Thomas."

"Hello, Josef. It's nice to see you again," Candy said, like she was greeting an old friend.

A deep, friendly laugh erupted from Felix. "It's nice to see you, also. I believe we have a little catching up to do."

That was an understatement if I'd ever heard one.

CHAPTER TWENTY-FOUR

By the time we were released by the police, it was after midnight. Mitch Raines had been the detective who caught the call and he hadn't been happy with me. He was going to have to get over it. I did what I thought was right, and the only thing I would change would be to have kept Rhonda from shooting Bruce. From all accounts, though, he was going to survive.

Candy insisted we come to her house after we were allowed to leave. Felix was going to join us. I was tired, but there was no way I was going to miss hearing what he had to say. When we arrived, Candy was in the kitchen making tea, and Tommy was pouring whiskey over ice into two glasses.

"Might as well make that three," Jake said.

"Splendid! How about you, Max?"

"None for me."

Jake followed Tommy to the kitchen to get another glass and some ice. Felix was studying the photos on the mantel.

"Do they bring back memories?" I asked.

He sighed. "Yes. It was so long ago, but sometimes it seems like yesterday." He turned around. "I apologize for being so gruff with you over the last two weeks. It was necessary."

I told him I understood, but I wasn't sure I did—at least not until I heard the whole story.

Jake, Tommy, and Candy returned to the living room. Candy poured tea for the two of us and we got comfortable. I sat on the sofa beside Jake and leaned into him.

Candy spoke first. "I don't mean to be blunt—"

I couldn't help it. I laughed.

"That's enough out of you, missy." She shook a finger at me and turned back to Felix. "Why are you in Pittsburgh? You're the last person I expected to see here—or anywhere for that matter. And where have you been all these years?"

Tommy interrupted. "Perhaps we should let Josef tell it in his own way, love."

"I'd appreciate that. But I will answer your first question," Felix said. "I was sent here on assignment last year."

"Assignment?" Jake said.

"Yes. I'm mostly retired now, but I've been with Interpol for many years. I've been tracking a series of art forgeries for the last few years, and after coming to many dead ends, a good lead brought me here."

"But you've been here for a year. Why did it take you so long?" I asked.

Felix smiled and glanced at Candy and Tommy. "The young are so impatient." He continued. "I needed to build trust with those involved. And the forgeries aren't always easy to spot. Doodle was extremely talented. With this latest piece, he fooled half a dozen experts. It takes time to produce a work of art to match the masters. Bruce and Rhonda didn't understand that. They pushed him to the limit and he'd finally had enough. He wanted to paint his own works, not copy someone else's. He was going to turn himself in. He made the mistake of telling Bruce he was done. And, well . . ." He didn't need to finish.

"What about Rhonda's husband?" I asked. "Did Bruce kill him, too?"

"I wasn't able to determine that," Felix said. "I'm hoping that Bruce will fill in some of these gaps when he recovers." He drained his glass and leaned back in his chair. "If that answers that first question, I have a tale to tell."

Boy, did he ever.

"I'm sure Catherine—I'm sorry—Candy, told you about what happened those last few months in Prague."

I nodded and Jake said, "Yes."

Felix stared at his hands then looked up at Candy and Tommy. "You thought that I'd betrayed you, and I thought that you'd betrayed me. It turned out it had been the KGB that had betrayed us all. I had worked hard for Dubček, helping to institute the few democratic reforms we could. When he was removed and Communists took power again, I didn't know what to do. I convinced the new government that I was on their side while still hoping things would change again. At least I had thought they were convinced. For a while I was able to feed correct information to you but the KGB became suspicious."

"What about the bug in our flat?" Tommy asked. "We assumed you placed it there."

Felix shook his head. "It wasn't me. I knew nothing about it until afterward. They had also placed a bug in my house. I believed that you had put it there."

Tommy got up and refreshed his drink. He held up the bottle. "Anyone?"

Jake shook his head but Felix handed his glass to Tommy and he refilled it.

Felix continued his story. "The night I found you, I was so angry. I had just found the bug in my house after being interrogated for hours about the raid on the empty building. They accused me of working with you. That I had passed word along to you that they were coming and that's why the building had been empty. I was going to make you both talk and tell me the truth."

Candy wiped tears from her cheek. "I could have killed you. I thought I did kill you. I am so sorry."

Felix nodded. "I am, too. I should not have been so angry. I knew how the KGB worked. I should have known it was them and not you. Can you forgive me?"

"There's nothing to forgive, old chap," Tommy said. "We were all just doing our jobs, and we're all here now. I suggest we let go of the past."

"Not just yet," I said. "What happened after you were shot?"

"I woke up in a hospital," Felix said. "The bullet had gone straight through my abdomen and luckily had missed any vital organs. Agents questioned me as soon as I was awake and accused me of helping you escape. They left a guard outside my door. I knew as soon as I was able to be moved, I'd be under arrest—a certain death sentence. I wasn't going to wait for that. My room was on the first floor and I escaped through the window. I made my way out of the country and eventually to France, which is how I ended up in Interpol."

"I wish I'd have known all this years ago," Candy said. "I should have tried to find out what happened to you. I thought about it many times, but part of me was afraid. There was always that little bit of hope that I hadn't actually killed a man. Killed you."

"No more regrets," Felix said. "I have a question for you, Catherine—I mean Candy. I can't get used to that. What is with the black and yellow clothing? I haven't seen you wear any other colors."

We all laughed, and Felix got his first lesson in Steelers Mania.

Friday morning and afternoon passed in a frenzy of getting the brew house ready for the beginning of the Oktoberfest weekend I'd planned for so long. While Jake spent the day in the kitchen, Daisy, Mom, and my sister-in-law, Kate, came to help us decorate. No easy feat with customers underfoot. At five p.m. I stood back and admired our handiwork. Blue and white streamers crossed the open rafters of the ceiling. We'd also hung a banner across the mirror behind the bar that read, *Welcome to Oktoberfest*. The centerpieces Daisy had put together looked great on the tables. The only thing that would be missing was the band. The Deutschmen were no more. I'd have to make do with the few German music CDs I owned.

I made a quick trip home to feed Hops and returned to the pub by six thirty. To my surprise, Felix and Manny were setting up in the corner. "I didn't expect this," I said.

Felix gave me a broad smile. "I know you hired a band, but I'm afraid you're stuck with just an accordion and a trumpet."

"It's really not necessary."

"It's the least we can do," Manny added. "I'm sorry I bugged out on you last night. That artsy stuff isn't my thing. But if I'd have known Bruce and Rhonda were going to pull something like that, I would have stuck around."

Shortly after that, the pub filled to capacity and soon it was standing room only. Nicole and I stayed busy behind the bar. The Oktoberfest beer I'd brewed using Kurt's recipe was a big hit, as was the Black Forest cake made from his recipe. I thought about how much he would have loved this little bit of Germany, and I missed him all over again.

Mom and Dad sat at one of the tables with Mike, Kate, and my nieces—who were very worried that Hops was home alone. I assured them she was fine and they'd see her on Sunday. Candy, Tommy, Daisy, Marcus, and Philip sat at another table, and when I was able to take a break, I joined them for a minute. I asked Philip how he was doing.

"I've been better," he said. "I'm afraid I'm going to lose everything over this. There will be an investigation to determine whether I acted in good faith."

"Felix will make sure you get a fair shake," Candy said. "You did your due diligence. It's not your fault your experts were wrong."

"Tell that to Victoria. I heard from her attorney already. She's suing me for two million dollars."

"Two million?" I said. "I thought she paid a million for the painting."

Philip grimaced. "The other million is for her so-called pain and suffering. Before she left, she made sure I knew how humiliated she was. She said she could never face anyone in this city again."

I hoped she included Jake and me in that.

"My attorney told me not to worry," Philip continued. "He said it would be Bruce and Rhonda who would be held liable."

The door to the pub opened, and Kristie and Vince came in. I excused myself and went to greet them.

"Good evening, Miss O'Hara," Vince said. "I hear you didn't take my advice to stay out of trouble."

"Good evening to you, Detective."

Kristie rolled her eyes. "Oh, for heaven's sake, knock it off, you two." She grinned and looked at me. "Or I'll tell him what you used to call him."

"You wouldn't!"

"Don't bet on it."

"Now I'm intrigued," Vince said. "What did you used to call me?"

"You'll never get it out of me," I said. I pointed across the room. "My parents are over there, and Candy and company are at the next table."

Kristie grabbed Vince's hand and pulled him in that direction.

Jake finally made it out of the kitchen, and I met him near the hallway beside the bar. "Come with me," I said. I put my arm through his and we snuck back to my office. I closed the door behind us. I wrapped my arms around his waist. "I thought it would be nice to have a minute alone."

He wiggled his eyebrows. "So you can have your way with me, I hope."

I laughed. "You wish."

He pulled me closer. "You bet I do."

My head rested on his chest, and I could hear his heartbeat.

"There's something I've been meaning to tell you," he said, "but it never seems to be the perfect time. And after last night, I realized there's never a perfect time, only the right time, and if I wait too long, there may be no time."

"Just spit it out, Lambert. You're not making any sense."

He reached under my chin and lifted my head. He looked so serious my heart began pounding. I thought about why he had to quit playing hockey and hoped it wasn't bad news. I couldn't take it. I held my breath.

"I love you, Max."

It wasn't bad news at all. It was great news. My heart swelled. I'd wanted to hear those words since—well, most of my life. I smiled through the tears in my eyes. "I love you, too, Jake. I always have."

"I know."

And then he kissed me.

RECITES

TURKEY SANDWICH
WITH CRANBERRY CHUTNEY

1 slice sharp cheddar
2 thick slices turkey
2 slices whole grain bread
Cranberry chutney

Place cheese and turkey on one slice of bread. Top with cranberry chutney, then add remaining slice of bread.

CRANBERRY CHUTNEY
2 cups fresh cranberries
1 jalapeño pepper, finely chopped

¼ cup sugar
¼ cup orange juice

Combine all ingredients in a saucepan and simmer for 10 to 15 minutes or until mixture thickens. Makes approximately 1½ cups. Refrigerate and use as desired.

HAM BARBECUES

Makes approximately 8 sandwiches.

2 lbs. Isaly's Chipped Chopped Ham, or other pressed
ham from the deli, sliced/chipped paper thin
1 28-oz. can tomato sauce
1 8-oz. jar sweet relish
½ cup brown sugar

Place all ingredients in a 6-to-8-quart slow cooker. Cook on low for 6 hours, or high for 3 hours. If you don't have a slow cooker, place ingredients in a large sauce pot and simmer on low heat for 1 hour. Serve on your favorite buns.

PITTSBURGH PRETZEL SALAD

BOTTOM LAYER
2 cups crushed pretzels
¾ cup melted butter
3 Tbsp. sugar

Preheat oven to 400 degrees. Mix all ingredients, and press into a 9-by-13-inch pan. Bake for 8 minutes. Cool.

FILLING (MIDDLE LAYER)

8 oz. softened cream cheese
1 cup sugar
1 8-oz. container whipped topping

Beat cream cheese and sugar until creamy. Fold in whipped topping. Spread over cooled pretzel mixture. Chill for 30 minutes or until Jell-O for the top layer is thickened.

TOP LAYER

2 3-oz. boxes strawberry Jell-O
2 cups boiling water
2 cups sliced strawberries

Combine Jell-O with boiling water. Stir until dissolved, about 2 minutes. Add strawberries. Chill until partially thickened, then spread over top of cream cheese mixture. Refrigerate overnight or until firm.

If desired, top with additional whipped topping and sprinkle with crushed or broken pretzel pieces.

BEER BRATS

8 to 10 bratwursts
1 sweet onion, sliced
1 bottle any kind of beer (or enough to cover brats)

Place bratwurst and onion in a large pan or deep skillet and pour in beer, making sure brats are covered. Simmer uncovered for 30 minutes. Drain. Return brats and onion to the skillet and brown to desired color. Serve with brown mustard on sausage rolls.

GERMAN POTATO SALAD

Makes 4 servings.

3 cups potatoes, cut into ½- to 1-inch pieces
(either with or without skins)
6 slices bacon
½ cup finely diced onion
¼ cup apple cider vinegar
3 Tbsp. sugar
2 Tbsp. water
Salt and pepper to taste
Parsley

Place potatoes in a pot of salted water and boil until easily pierced with a fork (about 10 minutes). Drain and set aside. Cook bacon in a skillet until crisp. Remove to paper towels. In the same skillet, add onion, vinegar, sugar, and water to bacon drippings. Cook until onion is clear. Add potatoes and crumbled bacon and mix. Season with salt and pepper to taste, if desired. Garnish with parsley and serve warm.

Keep reading for a special preview of
Joyce Tremel's Brewing Trouble Mystery,

TO BREW OR NOT TO BREW

Available now from Berkley Prime Crime!

ℐf looks could kill, the plumbing inspector giving me the bad news would have been in big trouble. "What do you mean there's a crack in the water line?" I said. "That's just not possible."

"Right here." He pointed. "You're going to have to replace this whole piece."

Sure enough, there was a one-inch gash in the line running to the brand-new stainless steel brew kettle, which we'd just installed a few days ago. I was hoping to brew a batch of pale ale tomorrow, but that was now out of the question.

The inspector brought me back down to earth. "You'll have to schedule another inspection after you get this taken care of."

This should have been the final plumbing inspection. The

brew kettle we'd been using had been a hand-me-down from a local brewery that had upgraded their equipment. I hadn't planned on a new brewing tank for another year, but this one had come up at a price I couldn't pass up. Everything else, from the kitchen to the restrooms to the tanks we'd installed previously, had all passed weeks ago. I couldn't afford a delay right now. The opening of my brewpub—the Allegheny Brew House—was only a month away.

"When I call to schedule it, how long will I have to wait until you come out?"

He shrugged. "I'll try to get out the same day, but it really depends on how busy I am."

That eased my mind a little bit—provided I could get the plumber in tomorrow to fix it.

The inspector passed a clipboard to me. "I need your signature that you acknowledge that you didn't pass."

I signed where he indicated.

He studied my John Hancock. "You don't look like a Max."

I'd heard that so many times, I'd lost count. I couldn't help it that I was born the only girl in my family. I had five older brothers and my parents assumed they'd have another boy when I surprised them twenty-nine years ago. My brothers all had normal first names—Sean, Patrick, Joseph, James, and Michael. I had no idea why they decided Maximilian would be a good name for a baby. It wasn't even Irish. Anyway, I ended up Maxine, but I preferred plain old Max.

"I'd get that fixed first thing tomorrow if I were you, Miss O'Hara."

As I watched him leave, I fought the urge to beat my head against the steel tank. All I could see were more dollar signs before my eyes. Although my plumber happened to be my brother Michael, he still needed to be paid. I got the family discount, but it was still money I hadn't planned on. Now I was second-guessing my decision to buy this tank.

"Another problem?"

I started at the sound of my assistant's voice behind me. Truth be told, Kurt Schmidt was more than an assistant. I didn't know where I'd have been without him. The son of one of my instructors in Munich, he knew just about all there was to know about brewing beer. He was also an accomplished chef who made the best apple strudel I'd ever tasted. He was easy on the eyes, too—tall, blond, and blue-eyed. There was no romance between us. He was more like my sixth brother, and he was completely devoted to his fiancée back in Germany. "I'd say so," I answered. "There's a crack in the water line." I showed it to him.

"That's very strange. It wasn't there yesterday," he said. "It should not have split like that. It is not a high-pressure line." He removed his wire-rimmed glasses and examined it closely. "Someone cut this."

"Impossible. No one's been near these tanks except the two of us. It was probably just defective."

"Do you really think Mike would have used a defective pipe?"

"Maybe he didn't see it." At this point, I was just relieved it wasn't a line that was turned on all the time. It might have flooded the whole pub.

"You don't think that any more than I do."

"There's no other explanation. Like I said, we're the only ones who have been near it."

Kurt put his glasses back on. "I suppose you still don't believe the loose electric breaker, the broken mirror, the scratched bar top, and the half dozen other little things aren't connected. I'm telling you, someone is trying to keep us from opening."

This wasn't the first time I'd heard this line of reasoning. Sure there'd been some minor annoyances, but they'd been bound to happen. Even during construction, things hadn't always gone according to plan. It went with the territory. There were always surprises. "You're right," I said. "I don't believe it." I turned and went down the metal stairs of the elevated platform that served to reach the higher sections of the tanks. I'd considered installing all the equipment out of sight, but decided half the fun of going to a brewpub was seeing how what you were drinking was made. I wanted a wall of glass, but because of the cost, I'd opted for a large window instead. Eventually, I planned to give brewery tours, but that was a long way off.

I went through the swinging wooden door of the brewery area, crossed the pine-plank floor, and sat down at the oak bar. I couldn't let myself believe we were being sabotaged. If I did, I'd be giving in to all those who said I'd never succeed in this endeavor. The first time I set eyes on the former Steel City Brewery, I knew it was what I'd been waiting for. When I returned to Pittsburgh from Germany after earning my brewmaster certification, I spent months searching for the perfect spot to open my brewpub. It had taken even longer to get financing, even though I had a nice inheritance from my grandmother for a down payment. No one wanted to take a chance on a five-foot-two female brewmaster. I finally found a lender that specialized in financing women entrepreneurs, and the rest, as they say, is history. At least I hoped so.

Seconds later, Kurt took the stool beside me. "It is not a coincidence."

"You don't know that," I said.

"Explain it, then."

"I can't any more than you can. Don't you think if someone was sabotaging us, they'd come up with something a little more elaborate? It's been annoying, but it's all fixable. And how are they getting in? None of the doors have been tampered with."

"That doesn't mean anything. Maybe whoever it is has a second career picking locks. At least the alarm company is finishing up soon. Then, when the alarm is set off, you'll see that I'm right." Kurt stood. "It's almost five o'clock. Why don't you go home? I'll lock up tonight. I want to work on that *kirschtorte* recipe."

"But it's delicious already." My mouth watered just thinking about it.

Kurt shook his head. "Not quite. It tastes like every other chocolate cherry cake. It's missing something. I want it to be perfect."

If it turned out half as good as the apple strudel, he could do whatever he wanted with it. The kitchen was his domain. I'd stick with the beer.

I took Kurt's advice for a change and left a short time later—after I called Mike, who promised to be there bright and early in the morning. Once outside, I turned to admire the building, like I did at least once daily. Sometimes I had to pinch myself to realize that all this really was mine. It was hard to believe that, not long ago, this had been an empty, forlorn shell. The former Steel City Brewery had been bought out by a large conglomerate, and the first thing the big boys did was shut down the Pittsburgh operation. All the equipment was auctioned off, and the buildings had sat empty for several years before the brewing plant itself had burned to the ground.

The single-story redbrick building, which was now the Allegheny Brew House, had been used as offices for the company. It was at the end of the row of buildings housing various shops and other businesses. It had taken quite a while to tear out everything down to the brick walls. I hoped my patrons would love the exposed brick inside as much as I did. A nice find had been pine-plank floors underneath the industrial linoleum. It had been much cheaper to have them restored than to install new boards.

Both the brewery and my loft apartment were in the Lawrenceville section of Pittsburgh. Since Children's Hospital had moved from near the University of Pittsburgh in Oakland to the Bloomfield-Lawrenceville border, the area was booming. It was no longer considered a "bad" neighborhood. Real estate values had skyrocketed, partly because of the medical professionals wanting to move close to work. Developers who bought up all the distressed properties and rehabbed them were likely making a killing on the resale. New shops and cafés opened constantly. It seemed like every time I walked up Butler Street to head home, I spotted something that hadn't been there the week before. On my block alone, there was a cupcake bakery, a flower shop, several boutiques, a deli, and a coffee shop.

I was tempted to stop for a treat when I passed the Cupcakes N'at bakery next door to the pub, but talked myself out of it. Out of towners always questioned the name of the bakery. The cupcake part they got, but inevitably someone wanted to know what *n'at* meant. I actually looked it up once and found it was short for *and all that*. Many of the expressions known as "Pittsburghese" originated with either the Scots-Irish or the Pennsylvania Dutch.

The owner, baker extraordinaire Candy Sczypinski, had become a good friend and apparently thought she was helping when she brought her creations over for us to sample, but my waistline couldn't handle much more. Between the cupcakes and other goodies, and sampling the menu items Kurt was coming up with, I was going to have to start walking more than just to the brewery and back. I considered joining the new gym a few blocks away, but I didn't know when I'd actually have the time to go.

Instead of a cupcake, I grabbed a turkey sandwich from the deli across the street. The deli was owned by Ken Butterfield, who manned the counter most days, but since it was after five, he was gone for the day. As I climbed the two flights of stairs to my apartment with my low-calorie sandwich in hand, I felt downright virtuous. That feeling was replaced with guilt when I unlocked the door. I'd moved here three months ago, but the place was still littered with boxes that I hadn't had time to unpack. I kept telling myself I'd get to them tomorrow, but after putting in twelve-hour days at the pub, I was too exhausted to do much of anything else.

But at least I had furniture. Sort of. Grandma O'Hara's traditional wingback sofa and chairs didn't exactly go with the modern style of the apartment. The dark mahogany end tables didn't match the bleached-oak laminate flooring. Gram's antique dining room set didn't even fit—it was stored in my parents' basement. It would have looked ghastly with the white cabinets and stainless steel in the kitchen anyway. She always said *Beggars can't be choosers*, and while I certainly wasn't a beggar, I was glad to have the hand-me-downs whether they matched or not. Besides, it was comforting to have a little part of her with me. I'd been in Germany when she passed two years ago, and I still regretted that I hadn't made it home for her funeral, although Gram herself would have been upset with me if I had. A waste of good money, she would have said. She'd never squandered so much as a dime. It was thanks to her that I'd had a nice down payment for the brewery.

When I finished eating my sandwich, I sat at the kitchen island and wondered what to do with myself. I wasn't used to this. I reached for the pen and pad beside the phone and made a list of things I had to do over the next week. The plumber was already taken care of. I had to schedule some waitstaff interviews. The alarm company needed to finish and activate the alarm. Kurt had already started training the kitchen staff, so I should probably touch base with how that was going. There were other miscellaneous deliveries that I needed to be present for. I hoped I wasn't forgetting anything.

The phone rang just then, and I picked it up.

"Wonder of wonders, my baby sister is at home." It was my oldest brother, Sean. Father Sean to his parishioners. Some people thought he had gone into the priesthood because he was the oldest Irish Catholic son, but it was truly a calling for him. He'd broken more than a few hearts when he decided on the seminary. We'd both inherited Mom's black hair and blue eyes, and they gave him a debonair movie-star look, especially when he wore the collar. If Hollywood ever remade *The Bells of St. Mary's*, he'd be a shoo-in to play Father O'Malley. Twelve years my senior, he was my favorite brother, although I'd never tell the others that. A little sister had been a novelty to him, and he became my protector from the day Mom and Dad brought me home from the hospital.

"You can always call my cell phone if I'm not at home, you know."

"I missed you at Mass yesterday," he said.

He obviously couldn't see me, but I felt my face flush anyway. I would have liked to tell him I went to another parish, but I couldn't very well lie to a priest, even if he was my brother. "Sorry about that. I got tied up at the brewery."

"You're working too hard. We missed you at dinner, too."

Sunday dinner was a long-standing family tradition. Most of the time I loved it. Since three of my five brothers were scattered across the country, Mom liked to keep the rest of us close. I often thought it was because Dad was a police officer. Even though he was a homicide detective now and not on the front lines as much as when he'd been in uniform, she still worried. I'd already talked to Mom that morning about missing dinner and she understood. At least, she'd told me she did.

"With the opening so close, I had a lot to do," I said.

"Anything I can do to help? Believe it or not, I haven't forgotten how to wield a hammer or a screwdriver."

"Don't let your parishioners know you can do that. You don't want the contributions to drop because they think you don't need to pay a handyman."

Sean laughed.

"Thanks for the offer," I said, "but we'll be fine if we stay on schedule. I'll be sure to make it to dinner next week."

"And Mass, too?"

"Hopefully."

"Maxie . . ."

Sean was the only one who dared call me that. When I was five, I busted the next-door neighbor kid in the chops for doing it. "Fine. I'll be there," I said.

"Good. I'll see you on Sunday."

I puttered around for a while and actually cleaned out a few boxes of kitchen items. It was nice to see the cabinets fill up. There was a small collection of German beer steins in one of the boxes, and I washed and arranged them on one of the built-in bookshelves in the living room. It was a nice touch, even though the rest of the shelves were almost empty. I vowed to make a better effort to get things unpacked. It was never going to look like home until I did.

By ten o'clock, I was tired and decided to call it a night. The phone rang as I finished brushing my teeth. I almost didn't answer it, and when I did, I was surprised to hear Kurt's voice.

"Is everything okay?" I asked.

"I was right."

"About what? Your *kirschtorte*?"

"No. The sabotage."

Not this again. "There is no—"

"Yes, there is. I know what's going on, and I know exactly who is doing it."

I would have argued more, but something in his voice stopped me. "What happened?"

"I have proof. I heard a noise and found . . . You need to come down here. It'd be better if I showed it to you. Then we can turn it over to the police and get to the bottom of this whole thing."

I still wasn't convinced anything was going on, but Kurt wouldn't have called this late if he didn't think it was urgent. So much for an early night. "I'll be right there."

"Kurt?" I called as I dropped my purse on the bar. The lights were all on, but he wasn't in the main room of the pub. Upset as he was, I thought he would have met me at the door. Maybe he was in the kitchen. I crossed the plank floor to the other side of the room and pushed open the swinging door. The scent of chocolate and cherries made my mouth water. His latest torte creation sat half-decorated on the stainless steel counter. A bowl of thickened tart cherries was beside it, along with a plastic piping bag that looked full of whipped cream. It was odd he'd walk away without putting it back into the refrigerator. I put the cherries and whipped cream in the fridge, then went looking for Kurt.

He wasn't in my office. I opened the door that led to the basement, but the lights were out. I stopped outside the men's restroom and knocked on the door. Twice. I didn't want to just barge in. Kurt was a good friend, but not that good. When he didn't answer, I peeked in. It was empty. I stood in the hallway and tapped my foot. I went back down the hallway to the pub. I could see through the window that the brewery was dark. Where could he be? Surely he wouldn't have taken off and left the place unlocked—especially after asking me to come down here. Could he have stepped out for a quick snack? I went back to the bar and sat down to wait.

Fifteen minutes later, Kurt hadn't returned. The longer I waited, the madder I got. Why had he bothered calling me if he was going to leave? Apparently, whatever he had to tell me wasn't all that important after all. I snatched my cell phone from my purse and tapped his number on the speed dial with a lot more force than I needed. He'd better have a good explanation. Seconds later, the sound of his phone ringing made me jump. The sound was muffled, so I couldn't figure out where it was coming from. I got up, and as I crossed the room the sound got louder. The ringing seemed to be coming from the brewing area. It didn't make sense that Kurt would leave his phone in the darkened brewery. I pushed the swinging door halfway open and paused. The ringing stopped, and Kurt's voice mail picked up. There was another sound, however—the mash tun was operating. A prickly sensation went down my spine. Why was that tank running? We had cleaned out the spent mash earlier when I'd brewed a batch of hefeweizen. There was no reason for it to be turned on, especially at this time of night.

"Kurt?" I fumbled for the light switch. My fingers found it and the overhead lights blazed on. I blinked a couple times at the sudden brightness and spotted Kurt on the platform bent over the large opening at the top of the mash tun. Something wasn't right about that. I was about to call his name again when it registered. His feet weren't touching the floor. Heart in my throat, I raced up the metal stairs, the clangs echoing through the room with each step. I reached for the switch beside the tank. My hands shook horribly. I missed the switch. I tried again and turned it off.

It wouldn't have mattered if I'd missed it again. There was a good reason why Kurt hadn't been waiting for me or responded when I called him.

He was dead.

Ready to find
your next great read?

Let us help.

Visit prh.com/nextread